WHITE WATER WIPEOUT!

Joe saw Frank about to pitch overboard, and he quickly grabbed his brother by the back of the shirt. He could see Oren and John reach for oars and begin to paddle frantically, trying to turn the boat around the right way before they hit a drop-off and a new set of rapids.

"Here, Joe!" Frank called out. He handed a pair of oars to his brother.

Before Joe could take them, the boat, caught in a fierce current, swung around a curve.

"Hang on, Joe!" he heard Frank shout as he lurched violently to the side of the boat.

The next thing Joe knew, he was flying out of the boat and into the swirling white water. The rapids buried him like an avalanche and dragged him under. . . .

Books in THE HARDY BOYS CASEFILES™ Series

Available from ARCHWAY Paperbacks

THE HARDY BOYS CASEFILES

NO. 82

POISONED PARADISE

FRANKLIN W. DIXON

AN ARCHWAY PAPERBACK
Published by POCKET BOOKS
New York   London   Toronto   Sydney   Tokyo   Singapore

AN ARCHWAY PAPERBACK *Original*

An Archway Paperback published by
POCKET BOOKS, a division of Simon & Schuster Inc.
1230 Avenue of the Americas, New York, NY 10020

Copyright © 1993 by Simon & Schuster Inc.
Produced by Mega-Books of New York, Inc.

ISBN: 0-671-79466-3

First Archway Paperback printing December 1993

10 9 8 7 6 5 4 3 2 1

THE HARDY BOYS, AN ARCHWAY PAPERBACK and colophon are registered trademarks of Simon & Schuster Inc.

THE HARDY BOYS CASEFILES is a trademark of Simon & Schuster Inc.

Cover art by Brian Kotzky

Printed in the U.S.A.

IL 6+

Chapter

1

"First they make rain forest cookies, then rain forest ice cream. Now it's a rain forest speech at the U.N.!" Joe Hardy whispered to his older brother. "When is it going to stop?"

Frank Hardy chuckled. "Not for a long time, I hope," he answered in a low voice, trying not to disturb the other onlookers packed into the balcony of the United Nations General Assembly. "This is just the first World Meeting on the Environment the U.N. has held, and the rain forest isn't the only part of the world that needs help."

"That's for sure." Joe's blue eyes scanned the crowded amphitheater below. Representatives from every corner of the globe were listening to a solemn official from Peru speak at the podium. "I could use some help myself, understanding what that guy's saying. He talks so fast."

"Just put on the headphones next to your seat, and you'll hear an instant English translation."

Joe slipped the headphones on and flipped the dial, overhearing snatches of Russian, Japanese, and French. "The statistics are even more confusing in English," he said, removing the headphones. "This guy's supposed to make us want to save the environment?"

"Ed will get everyone's attention," Frank whispered calmly. "He should be on next."

Relieved, the younger Hardy replaced his headphones and readjusted his six-foot frame in his upholstered blue seat to wait for Ed to come to the podium. Eduardo Yanomama had been a friend of the Hardys' since he had spoken at Bayport High School's Environmental Awareness Week the year before. Eduardo Yanomama wasn't Ed's real name. His tribe believed names to be sacred and forbade sharing them with outsiders, so Ed had invented a name others could use.

Joe had been impressed that the shy, dark-eyed college student was the son of a Yanomama Indian chief and had grown up in the rain forest of Venezuela. Ed had told them that the Yanomama had lived in the forest for thousands of years. Civilization was now threatening their way of life, and the tribe had sent Ed to the U.S. to learn American ways and to try to convince the American people to help stop the destruction of the rain forest.

As the speaker from Peru left the stage, the hall filled with applause. Joe joined in when he spotted Ed Yanomama, dressed in a suit and tie, making his way to the podium. At twenty-one, with jet black hair and bright, dark eyes, Ed seemed dignified and fearless. Representing his people was a big responsibility, Joe realized. If anyone could do it, Ed could, though.

"Members of the World Meeting on the Environment," Ed began, "as our friend from Peru has just informed us, the threats to the South American environment are many. One of the chief concerns for my people, the Yanomama, who continue to live in the forest, is the cattle industry. As many of you know, beef costs much less in South America than in the United States, and for this reason American restaurant chains have begun buying beef in record quantities from such countries as Brazil. Dreaming of huge profits, Brazil's cattle barons have already burned down enormous sections of the rain forest to clear grazing land for their cattle, creating a barren wasteland. This situation is growing worse every year—and now the desire for American dollars is causing the destruction to spread to my own native country, Venezuela."

Joe leaned toward Frank. "I'm beginning to wish I hadn't had that burger for lunch," he whispered.

"Shh!" Frank replied.

"If the rain forest continues to be destroyed at

this alarming rate," Ed continued, "the world will lose unimaginable riches—lifesaving medicines that come from its plants, the thousands of animal species that live within it, the many tribes that support themselves on its rivers, trees, and wildlife, and the oxygen it produces that helps fight global warming.

"All of us must learn to respect our mother, the great rain forest, before it is too late. She gives us life," Ed finished with great dignity.

He stepped off the podium, and the General Assembly exploded in applause.

Joe jumped to his feet. "Way to go, Ed!" He noticed many of the delegates were standing, too.

"That was awesome," Joe said, brushing the blond hair out of his eyes.

"There are still some closing remarks," Frank said as the applause died down. "Ed said we should meet him at a party they're having at a restaurant across the street. Maybe we should head over there now before it gets too crowded."

"Sounds good to me," Joe said. He tugged at his necktie, a bright green jungle print. "I'm even dressed for the part, thanks to that street vendor outside the subway station."

"Right," Frank joked, adjusting his navy blue blazer and striped tie. "You look about as dignified as a chimpanzee."

Outside, the New York City skyscrapers glistened above a fresh layer of snow, and the United Nations flags flapped and snapped in the raw December wind. Joe was glad he and Frank had taken the day to come to New York from Bayport to hear Ed speak, even if the trip did cut into their last precious week of Christmas vacation.

Even with a down jacket on, Joe was grateful it was only a short walk to the restaurant. The Hardys gave their names to the restaurant's hostess and were directed upstairs.

"I love New York parties," Joe said. He sensed the electric charge given off by the collected environmentalists, politicians, and Hollywood stars waiting for the arrival of the conference delegates. "Let's go see what they're serving. I bet it's very healthy. It looks like glowworms on toast from here."

"Glowworms are full of protein," Frank said, following Joe to the food table. "I hear they're almost as good for you as, say, fried cockroaches."

The Hardys barely had time to sample the assorted nut pastes on crackers, papaya slices wrapped in mint leaves, and cups of mango juice and coconut milk before Joe heard a familiar voice.

"Frank and Joe. There you are!"

Joe turned to see Ed Yanomama approaching them, followed by two taller men.

"I'm glad you could come," Ed said as he and the other two men joined the Hardys. Ed's dark eyes were bright with excitement. He stood a whole head shorter than Frank's six feet one inch.

"That was a great speech," Joe said.

Frank nodded. "I think you got through to a lot of people."

"Thanks. I hope so," Ed said. He turned to the two men who had joined them. "I'd like you to meet the detectives I told you about. These are Frank and Joe Hardy."

Ed gestured to the person next to him, a tall, silver-haired man. The man's face was as lined as a sixty-year-old's, but his body was that of a man in his thirties. "This is Oren Walker of the Iroquois nation. He teaches anthropology at Columbia University here in New York." Oren nodded and extended his hand.

"And I'm John Tsosie," the other man said. He was slightly taller than Oren, with jet black hair pulled back into a ponytail that reached to the middle of his back. He was wearing jeans and a tweed blazer.

"John is a sculptor and an elder of the Navajo nation," Ed said, obviously proud of his friend.

"An elder?" Joe asked, looking confused.

John laughed. "You can be an elder without being old. You just have to know something about the old Navajo ways."

"It's nice to meet you," Frank said. "How do you three guys know each other?"

"Through Maddie Hatfield. I may have told you about her," Ed said. "Her father is a cattle rancher in Montana. He wanted her to become a rancher, but she became a botanist instead. For the past eight years she's been studying the ways in which rain forest people use plants. She convinced my father to send me to America."

"Maddie has a talent for bringing people with the same interests together," John said.

Joe was impressed. "Is she here tonight?"

Ed frowned. "She was supposed to be. John has been staying in her apartment here in New York. She spends a lot of time in the forest or traveling, so she lets us use her apartment whenever we need it. But John hasn't heard from her in weeks, which isn't like her."

"You don't know where she might have been heading next?" Frank asked.

"Maddie takes part in environmental demonstrations around the country," John said. "She pickets toxic waste dumps and organizes boycotts. Most of her activities are supposed to take people by surprise, so Maddie doesn't talk about them in advance. But we did expect her to be at this conference because Ed was going to speak."

Ed stared at the floor, and Oren put a hand on his shoulder. "Don't worry," Oren said. "Maddie's strong. I'm sure she's all right." Then he tried to change the subject. "Tell me, how did two young people like you get to be famous detectives?" he asked Frank and Joe.

Before Joe could explain that he and his brother were just following the example of their father, Fenton Hardy, a flushed, plump young man elbowed his way up to the group. He was out of breath and sweating.

"Hey, guys!" he said, his eyes moving nervously from one of them to the next. "Did you hear the news?"

"Well, if it isn't Harvey Brinkman," John Tsosie said, his eyes narrowing. Joe noticed that Oren was frowning, and none of the men offered to shake hands with Brinkman. "I heard you might show up here. What news do you have for us? Your import-export business broke another record for profits in a single week?"

Brinkman grinned, ignoring John's sarcasm. "My business *is* doing brilliantly," he confided. "My little project with your people was just the beginning, my friend. It's South American curios that people want now, and I'm the man to bring them back."

"Brinkman visited John's tribe a few years ago," Oren Walker explained dryly to the Hardys. "He told the tribe they could make a fortune by mass-producing Native American crafts for him to sell. They worked fourteen hours a day for eight months. Then Brinkman paid them next to nothing and made enough for himself to become independently rich."

"I had to figure in my costs, Oren," Brinkman reminded the older man, his eyes widening in protest. "Why, if it weren't for me, John's tribe would still be on welfare."

"Many of them are, thanks to you," John snapped. "At least now we know to operate our own businesses."

"Well, then, we all profited," Brinkman concluded, giving the group a huge smile. He slapped Ed on the back, almost causing the smaller man to stumble. "We deal with native peoples all over the globe, Ed. In fact, I've been planning to send a couple of my development men into the forest to talk to your dad."

"Don't listen to him, Ed," John warned him. "In six months your people will be making macrame plant hangers, and by the time Brinkman leaves you alone again, your people will have forgotten how to hunt."

Joe noticed that Harvey seemed to be unfazed. "I don't expect you to understand," he said to John. "Anyway, the reason I came over was to tell you about a bulletin I heard on the radio. Did you know that Roger O'Neill's been kidnapped?"

"The president of Burgerworld?" Oren looked shocked. "You used to work for him, didn't you?"

Harvey nodded reverently. "He taught me everything I know."

"Excuse me," said Joe. "But are you talking about *the* Burgerworld—the fast-food chain with the great triple-decker cheeseburgers?"

"That's right." Brinkman beamed at Joe. "I did some advertising work for O'Neill right after

I graduated from college. Man, could that guy merchandize."

"What about the kidnapping?" Frank asked, intrigued by the story. "Where was he snatched?"

"In Caracas, Venezuela," Brinkman told them. "According to the radio announcement, I heard the police found his BMW idling empty on a street with the driver's door standing open."

"What was he doing in Venezuela?" Frank asked. He turned to Ed all at once. "Hey—is Burgerworld one of those cattle buyers you were railing against?"

"One of the worst," Ed said grimly. "O'Neill has many friends in the government and the cattle industry in my country. He has many enemies, too."

Just then, Joe noticed two men enter the room in identical blue jackets. He nudged his brother. "Hey, Frank, look. Those guys are FBI. They don't wear their official jackets in public unless they mean business."

"I wonder what they're up to?" Frank asked.

They didn't have long to wait for an answer as the two agents stepped up to the group and flashed their IDs.

"What's this all about?" Oren asked.

The taller of the two agents ignored Oren and focused instead on Ed. "Eduardo Yanomama, we're placing you under arrest for the abduction of Roger J. O'Neill," he said. "You have the right to remain silent—"

"Are you crazy?" Joe blurted out, staring first at the agent, then at Ed. "You can't arrest Ed. He wouldn't kidnap anybody!"

Joe felt his brother pull him back. "Not now, Joe," Frank whispered. "We'll deal with this the right way."

Joe knew his brother was right. Stunned, he and the others watched as the agents handcuffed Ed and led him out of the room. A shocked silence spread through the restaurant as other guests recognized the brilliant speaker from Venezuela.

"Don't worry, Ed!" Joe called to him. "We'll take care of this!"

His friend didn't look back.

Chapter

2

EVERYTHING, thought Frank, even the dirty blue paint, looks grim. He and Joe were seated in molded plastic chairs in the interview room of the Metropolitan Correctional Center, watching a guard watch them through big glass windows at one end of the room. It was almost five o'clock, about three hours after Ed's arrest, and the Hardys had been waiting for over an hour for Ed to be brought down from the maximum-security floor.

After the FBI agents had led Ed out of the restaurant, Frank had consulted with Oren Walker and John Tsosie about what they should do. The two men had gone with the Hardys to the Venezuelan consulate. There they were told that only Ed's lawyers and reporters on assignment would get to see Ed.

"Then we're in luck," Frank had said as the group left the building. He produced a pair of press passes stamped with his and Joe's names. "Ed had these sent to us so we'd be sure to get into the conference. He also told us to bring our passports for ID. I'd say Joe and I are set to see Ed at the M.C.C."

"That's great—*if* they believe you're reporters," Oren said skeptically.

"If Ed is branded a radical, it will be a blow to the whole movement to save the rain forest," John Tsosie explained to the Hardys. "Many organizations fall back on terrorist acts to generate publicity for their causes. So now the people who run the powerful foundations and interest groups run for the hills at any hint of violence. If they believe Ed is guilty, they'll cut off all aid to the Yanomama people. Give us a call at Maddie's later and tell us what happened," John finished.

Fortunately, the press passes did work. Frank and Joe had to surrender their wallets and keys to an armed guard at the M.C.C. The man then ushered them through a turnstile and up to an interview room, where Frank and Joe were locked inside.

"Ed must feel like a rabbit in a trap," Joe said, tapping one foot nervously. "Just being locked up in here for a few minutes is enough to make me want to organize a jailbreak."

Just then the guard spoke into a walkie-talkie,

and moments later a door opened at the opposite end of the room. Ed entered, led by another guard.

Ed still had on his dark suit, but Frank noticed that he also wore handcuffs attached to a chain at his waist. The Yanomama was pale even though he'd been in prison only a few hours. He did break into a wide smile as he saw the Hardys. When he sat down, the guard removed his handcuffs and left the room.

"How did you get in here?" Ed asked. "I didn't think I'd get to see anyone but the lawyer the people from the conference sent over."

"The power of the press," Joe said, brandishing his press pass.

"I wish it had the power to get me out of here," Ed said.

Frank could see how desperate Ed was. "Hey," he said optimistically, "no one could believe you had anything to do with this. Your arrest is causing a major uproar."

"I'm glad to hear I've got supporters," Ed said. "I'm in major trouble, Frank. The Venezuelan police claim they have hard evidence that I masterminded O'Neill's kidnapping."

"That's crazy!" Joe exclaimed. "What kind of evidence could it be?"

"The police found a dart tipped with curare on the floor of the backseat of O'Neill's car. Curare is a natural poison the Yanomama use for hunting. Just a little on an arrowhead can kill any animal. It paralyzes the central nervous system," Ed said.

"So what?" Frank objected. "Anyone could have planted it, to make it look like your people were responsible."

"It gets worse," Ed said. "They found a ransom note for a hundred million dollars, supposedly sent from the Yanomama of Venezuela. According to the note, my people plan to use the money to buy the land they live on and set up a rain forest preserve. The Venezuelan police claim that two Yanomama they brought in for questioning confessed that I masterminded the whole thing."

"But you weren't even in Venezuela," Joe said.

"Yes, I was," Ed admitted ruefully. "I went home when the Christmas holidays at college started so I could spend time with my father and my people. We went on a long trek called a *wayumi*. Several times a year my village goes off to look for new hunting grounds—to give the animals and plants a chance to come back to our old village. We were gone for almost two weeks. It was only yesterday morning that I flew to New York to speak at this conference. According to the police, O'Neill was probably kidnapped the day before I left."

"So the police believe you used the trek as a cover to double back and grab O'Neill," Frank said slowly.

"That's right," Ed said, desperation sounding in his voice.

"None of this makes any sense," Joe protested. "What was O'Neill doing driving around Caracas by himself? Wouldn't a guy that important have bodyguards, or a driver at least?"

"Ed, you said the conference people sent over a lawyer," Frank broke in. "What does he think?"

"He said the Venezuelan government is pushing to have me shipped back to stand trial as soon as possible." Ed looked sad, tired, and scared all at once. "A Yanomama doesn't stand a chance in a Venezuelan courtroom. Many people in the government still think we are wild and dangerous. They fear an educated Yanomama like me even more because they don't know what I'm going to do. There's no way I'd get a fair trial."

"Can't your lawyer do anything?" Joe demanded.

"He thinks he can keep me here for about a week while I ask for protection from your government," Ed told him.

"That was a good move," Frank said, sounding relieved. He added, "There's got to be something we can do."

"We can start by calling Dad," Joe suggested.

Ed smiled. "You're both great, and I appreciate your help," he said. "Believe me, I need all I can get."

"What about that scientist—Maddie—that you were talking about?" he asked Ed. She might have an idea who could have snatched O'Neill."

"How do we go about finding her?"

"That's a good question," Ed said. "I hope you will look for her. You could check her apartment. It's possible she left a note that we missed, telling us where she was going. She lives in Chinatown."

Joe jotted down the address as Frank leaned in close to Ed. "John said Maddie took part in a lot of demonstrations," Frank said.

"Yes," Ed said. "She even came up with the idea for the demonstration at Burgerworld headquarters here in New York a few years ago. It really got the word out about rain forest beef."

"Can you think of anything more for us to check out?" Joe asked. "Do you know who might have wanted to kidnap O'Neill and at the same time hates your people enough to frame them and you?"

Ed shook his head. "I don't know," he admitted. "I've been trying to think of who—" At that moment Frank saw a light dawn in Ed's eyes. "Wait—I just thought of something," Ed said. "O'Neill was probably in Caracas to talk to cattle ranchers about moving some of his business to Venezuela. From what I've heard, he's especially interested in buying from the Alejandros, a large clan of cattlemen who have already started cutting down the forest."

"But why would the Alejandros want to kidnap

O'Neill?" Joe protested. "He's the man who will make a fortune for them, right?"

"Exactly," Ed told him. The Alejandros have only one major enemy in Venezuela—the rival Da Silva clan. Enrique and José Da Silva, two brothers, make sure their family gets the best price for their cattle. They're a nasty pair."

"So you're saying the Da Silvas could hate O'Neill for giving the Alejandros business," Frank concluded. "Business they feel should be theirs. They might try to scare O'Neill into dealing with them. At the same time they could frame the Yanomama who want to stop them from clearing more land. We'll check out the Da Silvas."

Just then the door at the far end of the room swung open and a guard strode in. "Time's up, buddy," the guard said, roughly pulling Ed to his feet and handcuffing him. As he was pushed from the room, Ed twisted around and said, "Don't get in over your heads, you guys. If you need help, try to find Maddie."

Joe and Frank emerged from the Metropolitan Correctional Center into the blue December night and gulped deep lungfuls of cold air. "Ah, freedom," Joe said, stretching. "Frank, we've got to get Ed out of that place."

"Let's start by finding Maddie," Frank said. "If she's not at her apartment, we may be able to figure out where she went. Maybe Oren and John can help us. They told us to call, but I think we should just stop by there."

Frank fell into step beside Joe, and the two walked north, past a huge, columned courthouse covered with snow-capped statues.

"What do you think the story is with this Maddie?" Joe asked. "It sounds as if she would hate O'Neill."

"I can understand why," Frank remarked. "I'd count her as a suspect in O'Neill's kidnapping. What I find hard to believe is that she would frame the Yanomama. Much less Ed."

"So where is she?" Joe asked. "According to Ed, she's been his guide in this jungle." He threw out his arms to indicate the dark streets. "I wonder why she didn't contact him if she couldn't make it to the conference."

Frank shrugged. "I guess we'd better find out. After we check out her apartment, let's get some Chinese food, okay? I'm hungry—which means you must be practically dead of starvation."

Just then Frank spotted Harvey Brinkman, the young businessman who had given them the news of O'Neill's kidnapping, around a corner and under a streetlight about fifty feet in front of them. The man's eyes brightened when he saw the Hardys, and he hurried up to them, his expensive raincoat open and flapping at his sides.

"We've met, of course," Brinkman said, holding out a soft, warm hand. "But I'm afraid I didn't get your names."

"Joe Hardy, and this is my brother Frank."

"I guess you went to the M.C.C. to talk to Ed," Brinkman said. "I'm heading there now to see if there's anything I can do to help."

"I don't think they'll let you in," Joe said. "Unless you can prove you're his lawyer or a reporter."

"I shouldn't have a problem gaining entry," Brinkman said with a confident laugh. "I'm not without resources, you know. So, where are you two headed? Maybe after I've chatted with Ed, we can have dinner. My business dinner was canceled, and I know a wonderful Chinese restaurant—"

"We'll have to pass," Frank said. "We have to get somewhere."

Harvey smiled affably. "Another time then, I hope," he said. "I'll be seeing you."

"Why did you turn him down?" Joe asked Frank after Harvey strode away through the snow. "He seems like a nice guy. If you ask me, Oren and John were really hard on him."

"First, Oren and John probably know him better than we do," Frank replied. "Second, we're supposed to be searching Maddie's apartment. And third, someone knows Ed Yanomama well enough to want to frame him—and that someone could just as easily be one of Ed's contacts in New York as a cattleman in Venezuela."

Within minutes Frank and Joe entered New York's Chinatown district. The air was filled with the pungent odors of spices, oranges, and roast duck. All shop signs were in Chinese as well as English. Even the phone booths had tiny pagoda tops.

The two brothers turned left down tiny Pell Street, their stomachs growling as they inhaled the delicious aromas of a Chinese dumpling house. Frank noticed that the street was deserted, as if the residents had surrendered the sidewalks to the bitter chill of the December wind.

"Maddie's apartment should be at the end of the street," Joe said, double-checking the address Ed had given them. "Let's find her apartment, then go dig into some steamed dumplings. Maybe I'll have them sprinkled with ginseng or lizard dust or something to give me energy."

Joe wasn't watching and bumped into a tall man in a black leather jacket who had appeared out of the shadows near the end of the street. Frank peeked past him and saw two other tall young men, one in a denim jacket and one draped in what looked like a Native American blanket. They were huddled in the dark entrance of an apartment building, and Frank couldn't see their faces.

"Oh—excuse me," Joe said, pulling back from the man he'd accidentally bumped. The man said nothing, only stared at Joe. An uneasy feeling crept over Frank. Glancing behind him, he saw that the street was still deserted.

"Hey, man, that's okay," the young man finally

said, circling around the Hardys so that he blocked their exit. "You're looking for Chinese food?"

Turning to face the stranger, Frank involuntarily took a step back. His brother did the same.

"I know a special place tourists don't know about," the man said with a mysterious grin. "It's right behind you. Turn around." The man made a circling motion with his index finger and stepped forward again, backing the Hardys closer to his two companions in the entryway.

Frank and Joe traded a quick look, long enough to read the question in each other's eyes. Were they being mugged?

Frank knew Joe wouldn't take any chances. As the stranger advanced on them again, the younger Hardy shouted, "You picked the wrong guys to jump, pal!" Before Frank could stop him, Joe took a swing at the tall man.

"Hey!" the tall man yelled, his surprise showing on his face. He blocked Joe's punch and drilled a fist into Joe's stomach. "Look out!" Frank shouted too late. Joe staggered backward and crashed down a flight of basement stairs, Frank clattering after him.

Chapter

3

JOE CRASHED into a heavy metal door at the bottom of the stairway with a bone-jarring thud. The world went fuzzy as Joe tried to shake the cobwebs out of his head. He felt a heavy grip on his shoulders and focused on Frank's worried face.

"Joe!" Frank said, shaking his brother. "Are you okay? Say something."

"Watch that first step," Joe muttered as Frank helped him to his feet. "It's a killer."

"Are you two all right?" called a voice from the top of the stairs. Joe glanced up and saw the man who had slugged him. Concern was etched on his face. "Sorry about the punch—it was pure reflex."

"If you guys are finished, I'll buzz you in at

the entrance and you can come up to Maddie's loft," called out another voice, which Joe recognized as Oren Walker's.

Confused, Joe ascended the basement stairs, Frank right behind him. On the top step Joe glared at the guy who'd punched him. "Who are you?" he demanded.

"I'm a friend of Ed's," the man replied. "I came here to Maddie's hoping to find a clue or something to help him—like you guys."

Joe glanced over the man's shoulder and saw that one of the men in the doorway was John Tsosie. The sculptor was wearing the Native American blanket coat. John shook his head and smirked at Joe. "I hope the elevator is working," John joked. "You don't seem to be very good with stairs."

"Very funny," Joe retorted.

"Look," the tall man said, extending his hand, "no hard feelings, okay? Chinatown can be a dangerous place. I don't blame you for over-reacting."

Joe accepted his hand. "Ditto," he muttered.

"I'm Sogyal Lalungpa. Of course, you know John," the tall man said, motioning toward his friends. "The gentleman with him is Matt Von Brocklin."

Joe studied Sogyal and Matt. They were both about the same age, in their early twenties. Sogyal was tall and rugged with jet black hair and high, wide cheekbones. Matt was tall and lean with sandy hair and a spray of freckles across his face.

"Let's get inside," Sogyal suggested. "We'll put some ice on that head of yours."

Joe and Frank followed the trio into the building and sandwiched themselves into a decrepit elevator that protested all the way to Maddie's floor, where it jarred to a stop. As the elevator doors opened, Joe saw Oren standing beside an open door.

"Come on inside, guys," Oren announced. "I ordered food, in case anyone's hungry. Should be here soon."

The guy's a mind reader, Joe thought. Even a tumble down a flight of steps hadn't ruined Joe's appetite. If anything, he was hungrier than ever.

Oren led the Hardys into the rosy light of a wide, spacious loft. Joe scanned the place, noticing the overstuffed furniture and rows of bookshelves that took up a good third of the wall space. A small computer station was set up in a far corner.

What caught Joe's eye was a stone sculpture in the center of the room. It was a warrior on horseback. Joe thought the sculpture was sad and fierce at the same time.

"John made that," Oren said.

"Wow—you're really good," Joe said, turning to John.

"Let's all sit down together," Oren said. He led them to the back of the room and a long oak table. It was set for six. Beyond the table, visible through an open swinging door, was a small kitchen.

"I'll be back in a second. I'm going to get ice for Joe's head," John said, disappearing into the kitchen. Walker pulled out a chair and sat down, and the others followed his example.

There was a knock at the door. "Food's here," Matt said cheerily, standing up and marching over to the door.

"What's going on here, Oren?" Frank asked.

"We were going to meet here to decide what to do about you two," Oren said, seeing the curiosity that burned in the Hardys' eyes. "You boys have proved yourselves so committed to helping Ed that John and I decided back at the M.C.C. to tell you about our group. Now that you're here, we want you to sit in."

"Sit in on what? What group?" Joe demanded.

Oren smiled. "I'm getting to that, Joe." He leaned forward in his chair as Matt approached with several white bags of aromatic food. "The group was put together a couple of decades ago by Native American elders and chiefs, but now we have members all over the world."

"We call ourselves The People," Sogyal interjected. "We have members from Australia to Alaska—from aborigines to Eskimos to the Yanomama to European Americans like Matt and Maddie."

"So Maddie's a member," Frank replied thoughtfully.

"And, Ed," Matt said, passing out dishes and silverware. "We're more like a group of friends than an organization. We're committed to helping save the environment wherever it's threatened. What we have in common is the belief that we can't help the Earth unless we learn from the ways of native people."

"That's right," Sogyal said. "If the rain forest is destroyed, we'll lose more than plants and animals. We'll also lose all the knowledge that the native people there have shared for centuries."

Joe was impressed. "It sounds like what you're doing is important," he said.

"Well, there aren't a lot of us," Oren said. "People come and go. We now have maybe thirty or forty members scattered around the world. What we're trying to do is encourage native people to hang in there and keep up the old ways, the old knowledge. People like the Yanomama have a lot to teach the rest of the world."

Just then John emerged from the kitchen, carrying a tray of glasses, a pitcher, and an ice pack.

Joe accepted the ice pack gratefully. "Thanks, man," he said. "Now that my head's taken care of, I can think about my stomach."

Matt laughed and opened the cartons of steaming dumplings, sesame noodles, and trays of rice and spicy shredded beef. They all helped themselves.

"So where do you think Maddie is?" Joe asked after everyone had finished. Sogyal shrugged as did Oren, Matt, and John. "Look, you know her. She's a member of this group. You must have some idea where she could be."

"We told you that Maddie likes to take part in demonstrations," Oren said. "The rest of us are wary about getting arrested to prove a point. We don't think it's the best way to help our people. Maddie respects that, so she doesn't tell us what she's up to."

"Ed seemed to think Maddie might be able to lead us to O'Neill's kidnappers," Joe told him.

"Do you mind if we take a look around?" Frank asked.

"Go ahead," Oren said. Frank headed for a cluttered desk that stood in an alcove on the opposite wall. Joe joined him and they started flipping through the thick stack of newspaper clippings and lab reports on the desk.

A moment later Frank picked up a thick manila file. "What's this?" he asked, opening the file. Joe saw that it was filled with more newspaper articles. Most of these were accompanied by gritty photographs of a young, bearded man brandishing a variety of automatic weapons.

"His name is Carlos Cruz," Joe said, reading one of the captions. "According to these articles, he's a revolutionary turning Venezuela upside down."

"Ah, yes, Carlos Cruz." Oren sighed as the

Hardys returned to the dining table with the file. "He's the leader of an ultraradical guerrilla group. They're trying to overthrow the government in Venezuela by winning converts among the peasant population."

"His group calls itself the Red Shirts," John said. "They hate all rich cattlemen who pay the workers nothing. Sometimes the Red Shirts dump kerosene in streams to poison cattle. The problem is, it also kills the fish the Yanomama eat, so that if they eat poisoned fish they die. Maddie and Ed can't stand him."

"So he hates the cattlemen and he's an enemy of Ed's," Frank said, thinking out loud. "He'd be a perfect suspect in the O'Neill kidnapping, wouldn't he?"

Oren frowned thoughtfully. "It's an interesting idea," he admitted. "A hundred million dollars would buy a lot of bullets."

"But doesn't he want the Yanomama on his side?" Joe asked. "They've been oppressed by the cattlemen, too."

"He has won over some of the natives from other tribes," John told him. "But he hasn't had much luck with the Yanomama. Ed keeps reminding them that Carlos and his rebels don't care about the land. He tells the Yanomama to stay away from Carlos and his revolution."

"So by framing Ed for the kidnapping, Carlos could kill two birds with one stone," Frank said.

"Right!" Joe said. "He takes out O'Neill, gets

a ton of money, and gets rid of Ed, all at the same time."

"There's something about it that doesn't sit right with me," Oren said. John got up to clear the table, waving away Frank's offers of help. "A rebel group like the Red Shirts likes to take credit for all its terrorist actions. Carlos likes to send big, loud messages to the world. I think he'd tell everyone he had O'Neill."

"Then who else hates both O'Neill and the Yanomama?" Frank asked.

"Ed mentioned the Da Silva brothers," Joe said. "The Da Silvas may have nabbed O'Neill when it looked like he was going to pay a rival clan to supply Burgerworld with beef."

"Better for both clans to stay poor than for Da Silva's rivals to get rich," Frank explained. John set out bowls for ice cream and sat down. Frank stared first at Walker, then at John. "Here are my questions then. Where is Maddie, and why is she so interested in Carlos Cruz?"

"If you're thinking she's in with this revolutionary group, you're wrong," John said. "She may be radical but never violent. And she would never betray Ed."

Joe was starting to get impatient. "We can't get any answers sitting here in New York."

"That's why we're meeting," Oren said. "To come up with a plan."

"Speaking of plans, are you two guys heading uptown or where tonight?" John interjected, scowling at Oren. Joe realized that John wasn't willing to let the Hardys in on the details of The People's plans. Nothing more would be said then. Joe also realized that it was late and neither Frank nor he had given a thought to where they'd stay. They had planned to take the train home to Bayport right after the party for Ed.

"I guess we should call our dad," Frank said.

"Why don't you come uptown with us and call your dad from my apartment?" Oren suggested to the Hardys, waving John away. "If you want, you can sleep on my floor and catch a train back to Bayport in the morning."

"Sogyal and I will stay here," Matt said with a significant look at Oren. "That way we can take a message if Maddie calls."

That settled, Joe, Frank, Oren, and John left Maddie's building and stepped out into the cold night. Chinatown was like a carnival. The sidewalks were so crowded that the group had to walk single-file.

On the walk to the subway Joe wondered how Ed was doing. He also wondered where O'Neill might be imprisoned—if he were alive. As the group walked down the steps to the subway at Canal Street and East Broadway, Joe wondered which would be worse—to be imprisoned as a kidnapper, or to be imprisoned by one.

After they pushed through the subway turnstiles and made their way to the platform, Joe walked to the edge and looked down at the sooty subway tracks. "I always wondered why that far third rail stays so shiny when the other two are black," he said to the others.

"Hear that buzz?" John asked. "That's the third rail humming. It carries the electricity that runs the subway cars, and it can fry anything that touches it."

A train rumbled in the distance. Joe leaned forward to see the train make its way out of the dark tunnel. At the other end of the platform, Joe saw a man wearing a raincoat and carrying a briefcase hurry up the platform. He must be running late, Joe thought absently. As he drew closer, Joe noticed that a black ski mask covered his face.

Joe turned to his brother. "Hey, Frank—" he began, but John interrupted him.

"Watch it!" the sculptor yelled as the masked man pushed past him. Joe spun around, his eyes widening as the man raised and swung his briefcase, clipping Joe on his head.

In what seemed like slow motion Joe felt himself pitching backward. He saw Frank and the others ignore the fleeing assailant and lunge, arms outstretched, toward him.

Joe was hurtling down into the soot-blackened well of the tracks, down toward the buzzing third rail and instant death.

Chapter

4

"JOE!" FRANK SCREAMED. His voice was almost drowned out by the earsplitting squeal of emergency brakes. Joe had landed hard in the train bed on his right side, his face inches from the third rail. Before he could get to his feet, Frank had leapt down beside him and was helping him to the side. The train skidded toward them, huge and deafening, as Oren reached down from the platform.

Joe and Frank hoisted themselves up the side of the platform with Oren's help as the train came to a shrieking stop—about a car's length past where they stood.

As the crowd erupted in cheers, a young blond police officer broke through the crowd, escorted by John. Frank could see that John was winded.

"I tried to catch him," John said, panting. "He had too much of a lead on me. Man, am I glad you're all right."

"Someone pushed me," Joe told the officer. "I almost got fried."

"Your friend told me. Did you get a look at the guy?" the officer asked. Joe shook his head, bending down to spit soot from his mouth.

"He was wearing a ski mask," Joe said, rubbing his head. "And it felt like he was carrying a briefcase full of bricks."

"There are millions of guys in this town who wear trench coats and carry briefcases," Frank said, exasperated. "All he had to do to blend in with the crowd was toss the ski mask. He could be right here, and we wouldn't even know it."

As Frank spoke, a rescue team arrived on the platform. Once the paramedics had cleaned Joe up a little, he was escorted aboveground by two officers, along with Frank, Oren, and John. Frank noticed the relieved expressions on the commuters' faces surrounding them.

"And they say New Yorkers don't care," John said with a smile.

"Just wait fifteen minutes," said the young blond officer. "They'll be complaining about the train running late." He nodded at John. "By the way, this longhair here ran his heart out."

"Yes, but I lost the guy," John said with a downcast look. "I must be getting old."

"At least you tried," Frank said. "The rest of us just freaked out."

After talking with the officers for another five minutes, Oren suggested they take a taxi to his Upper West Side apartment. They caught one easily, and soon were moving slowly through the majestic man-made canyons of towering skyscrapers. The snow had slowed traffic somewhat. In midtown the sleek gray towers glowed against the night sky. High atop one modern glass-box building, Frank spotted the Burgerworld corporate logo: an electric blue B inside a globe. He found himself wondering about the man who so badly wanted to put his mark on the world that he didn't mind burning down the rain forest—and destroying the people who lived there.

Frank turned to Oren and John. "Tell us what you know about Roger O'Neill."

"I don't know much, but I hear he's pretty nasty," Oren said. "Maddie says he's paranoid, always accusing people of being after him."

"Right," John said. "I remember reading that he grew up poor in a small town in upstate New York. His little brother was a real whiz kid who got a full scholarship to Harvard. Roger didn't get to go to college at all. According to the article, Roger's dad used to say that Roger would spend his whole life flipping burgers. Well, he did—right into a huge empire."

"Maybe we should try to talk to O'Neill's

brother," Joe suggested. "He might know something about what Roger was up to in Venezuela."

"Can't talk to him," John said. "He became a famous anthropologist, but ten years ago he disappeared on a trip up the Amazon. Nobody in his party came back."

The car turned at Seventy-sixth Street to enter Central Park. The trees looked dense in the darkness, and the old-fashioned cast-iron street lamps were haloed with fog. Moments later the taxi exited the park again and soon stopped in front of a brownstone on West Ninety-sixth Street. There, Frank and Joe followed Oren and John up three flights of stairs to a small apartment filled with books, Native American pottery, baskets, and rugs.

"All right, time's up," Joe said as Oren sank into an overstuffed easy chair in his living room. "Ed's been in custody a few hours already, and so far none of us has done anything to get him out. I think we're wasting our time hanging around New York City. We need to go to where the crime was committed—Caracas, Venezuela. If we're going to catch the real kidnapper, that's the place to start."

"What do you mean, we?" John demanded from the sofa. "What can you do in Caracas? The police won't talk to you, and you're sure not going to get anywhere with a bunch of cutthroat cattlemen."

"Exactly," Joe said with a triumphant glance

at his brother. "That's why you two will have to go along. That's your secret plan, anyway, isn't it? To go to Venezuela, catch the kidnapper, and force the authorities to free Ed?"

John and Oren traded looks.

"They know, John," Oren said with a philosophical shrug. "There's not much point in denying it now."

John scowled. "We have to go. Ed is one of us—and a close friend of mine. I'd no sooner leave him in that jail than cut off my own hand."

"That's how we feel, too," Frank said, stepping forward eagerly. "We haven't been friends with Ed for long, but we'd do anything to help him."

"In one way I'm even more involved in this than you are," Joe pointed out. "Somebody tried to kill me on that subway platform."

"Also, Ed asked us to find Maddie Hatfield," Frank added with a note of finality. "And I bet she's in Venezuela."

"Right," John said dryly. "The only problem is, Maddie would be in the rain forest."

"So what?" Joe demanded. "We'll go in and get her."

"You?" John stared up at Joe, aghast. "You think that place is like a public park? I fought in Vietnam, kid, and I would have a rough time trekking through that terrain."

"But you're planning on doing that, aren't you, John?" Joe said.

"No," Oren interjected. "We're planning on

contacting a friend of mine in Caracas. We hope she might be able to help us find Maddie. We have no intention of venturing into the rain forest alone."

"Unless we have no other options," John added. "There's no way you could come along, though. You wouldn't last a day."

"We're in good shape," Joe said, offended.

Frank hesitated. Joe was being impulsive, as usual, but he had a point. They had to help Ed. "Joe and I are going to Venezuela with or without you," he announced. "It's up to you."

"Determined, aren't you?" Oren said with a grin. Joe and Frank nodded. Oren glanced quickly at John, then said, "Okay, come with us. Provided you stick with us and do what we tell you, and provided you clear it with your family."

John moaned and closed his eyes.

"You can use the phone in the kitchen," Oren added.

Joe turned to Frank. "Leave this to me. I'll make sure Dad won't turn us down."

Joe found the phone, and Frank paced the small room, reading book titles in the bookcases and examining wooden masks and a beautiful, desert-colored rug that hung on the wall. Above Oren and Walker's low-voiced conversation, Frank could hear Joe talking in the next room.

"Everything's set," Joe called, hanging up the phone. "Dad wants us to call him when we can and get back in time for school."

"Great," Frank said, feeling his pulse quicken. Suddenly everything was happening very fast. He sat on the sofa next to John. "Now you can tell us everything," he said to Oren. "For starters, how do we get to Caracas?"

"We'll be flying in a private plane first thing tomorrow morning," the professor told him.

"That's where Matt fits in," John added. "He's our pilot. Matt and Sogyal are going to pack the equipment we'll need tonight and get out to Kennedy Airport at dawn."

"We're hoping to stay with an anthropologist I know in Caracas—the friend I mentioned earlier," Oren said. "Only she doesn't know it yet, so I'd better call her."

Joe sank down on the edge of a chair as Oren headed toward the kitchen.

A few minutes later Oren reentered the living room, shaking his head. "Elena said the Venezuelan police are treating the case like a national emergency." He turned to Frank and Joe. "Hey, I hope you guys have passports."

"We used them for identification at the U.N.," Joe said.

"Great. So all you need is everything else," Oren said with a chuckle.

With Oren and John's help, the Hardys quickly filled a borrowed duffel bag with T-shirts, towels, a pair of toothbrushes, and other odds and ends. "This is cool," Joe said when they had packed everything they thought they would need. "If I ever find myself stranded with dirty teeth and no insect repellent, I sure know who to call."

"Oren's the world's biggest packrat," John told the Hardys.

Just then the intercom buzzed, interrupting their conversation. "Who could be at the door at this time of night?" Oren wondered out loud.

Crossing the room to a speaker unit near the front door, Oren pressed the button and called, "Who is it?"

"That's strange," he said after a moment of silent waiting. "Nobody's there."

"Let's check it out," Frank said, instantly on the alert. He led the others downstairs to the front of the building. Cautiously pulling the front door open, he peered up and down the street but saw no one. What he did see was a small steamer trunk on the front stoop. Frank squatted in front of it and tried one of the clasps. It was locked.

"Boy, talk about suspicious," Joe said. "There could be a bomb or something in there."

Joe was right. The sense of danger Frank felt made his hearing and sight supercharged.

"Let's not get paranoid, guys," John said. "It's probably just our supplies. Sogyal and Matt might not have had room to take this to the airport for us. Come on—let's carry it upstairs."

"They were in such a big hurry they couldn't stay to talk?" Oren said, huffing as he helped John carry the trunk upstairs.

"I guess so. Let's open it and see." They

dropped the trunk inside the apartment near the front door. John disappeared into the kitchen and returned a moment later with a hammer and screwdriver. He raised his arm to bash open the clasps of the trunk.

"Wait a sec, John," Frank said, closing the apartment door behind him. "What if it *is* rigged?"

"You guys are too much." John laughed. "You want to dunk it in the tub and ruin our supplies?"

With that, John brought his arm down, smashed the lock, and threw open the lid. There was a deep sound and then a sickening thud as an arrow fired from a crossbow mechanism inside the trunk plunged into John's chest.

Chapter

5

FRANK DIVED to catch John when the arrow hit, but the older man went flying from the impact, hitting the apartment wall. He slid to the floor, unconscious, his hand wrapped around the arrow that had pierced his chest. There was no blood. Oren made him comfortable on the floor.

"John!" Joe said, kneeling beside the prone man. "Hang in there! We're calling an ambulance." Before Joe could make the call, John struggled and sat up with Oren and Frank supporting him.

"My chest," John said in a whisper. "It feels like it's on fire." Oren fumbled with the button on his friend's shirt just above the arrow. John then slid the arrow out. A round metal locket was now embedded in its tip. Oren undid the clasp holding the chain and slid it off. On John's chest, where the locket had been resting, there was a round red welt that seemed to be swelling.

"What's that?" Oren asked.

"It was a gift from Sogyal," John said with a rasp that was supposed to be a laugh. "Tibetan warriors wear these. You're supposed to put sacred objects inside, just like you do in a medicine bundle."

"So, what have you got in there?" Frank asked. "Kryptonite?"

"Actually, it's a piece of lead," John said. "A medic dug it out of my shoulder in Vietnam. A piece of shrapnel."

"Powerful medicine, that charm." Oren laughed. "Of all the places the arrow could have hit—this was the only one that would spare your life."

"What a dumb mistake," John said, embarrassed. "I should have listened to you. I'd be dead now if it weren't for Sogyal and his gift."

"The good news is it's just going to be a nasty bruise," Oren said, closing John's shirt. "It looks like you'll be flying with us tomorrow."

Joe paced the room. "This is too much," he said. "Two attacks in one night."

Oren picked up the arrow and examined it. "I've got more bad news. I'm guessing that this is a Yanomama arrow. There's some sticky resin-like stuff on the tip that I'm pretty sure is curare."

"Someone is definitely trying to frame the Yanomama," Frank said.

"We'll get to the bottom of this," Joe added, determined. "Next stop, Caracas."

The next morning was a blur of shopping and packing. John stayed in the apartment while Oren took Frank and Joe out shopping for tropic-weight pants, light hiking boots, and any other supplies he hadn't been able to provide the night before. Frank also picked up a copy of the *New York Times* from a newsstand. When they got back to the apartment, John was just finishing packing a first-aid bag, including the all-important antimalaria tablets, Camoprim.

"Malaria is carried by the anopheles mosquito," Oren explained. "Back in the fifties the Yanomama were so isolated there was no malaria. The year after they were exposed, thanks to an explorer who came up the Orinoco looking for lumber, half the population died. They were dying so fast there was no one to cut firewood for funeral pyres."

"You don't want to get malaria," John said. "I've had it. I remember shaking like a leaf in a storm—weak as a kitten for weeks."

Joe shuddered. "I hope those mosquitoes keep their distance," he said.

Frank was busy studying the newspaper, and Joe was peeking over his shoulder. "Hey, look, there's O'Neill," Joe said. There was an article about the kidnapping and a picture of the burger baron on the front page. Joe studied the picture. O'Neill had thin, dark features and wore horn-rimmed glasses.

"It says here that O'Neill's family is glad Ed was arrested," Frank said. "They're hoping that when the Venezuelan police get hold of him, he'll reveal where O'Neill is being held. It also mentions O'Neill's brother, the one who disappeared in the rain forest." After reading the article out loud, he folded the paper and stuffed it in his duffel bag.

"Let's get out of here," Oren said. "Matt and Sogyal are waiting for us. We're hours behind schedule already."

They reached the airport in less than an hour. Matt grinned and waved when he saw them, then greeted Oren and John with a high-five. Sogyal smiled but was more subdued.

"Frank, Joe, glad to see you. Oren called to let us know you were coming. Let's move it, now," Matt added. "We only get to park these private heaps at Kennedy overnight, and I've been here over twenty-four hours. Do you guys feel brave?" he asked, turning and grinning at Frank and Joe.

"Matt's been The People's pilot since he got out of flight college in Daytona, Florida, about three years ago," Oren said. "We keep the plane on an airstrip in Navajo territory."

"Yeah," Matt said, patting the plane. An eagle feather was painted on the side. "I found this big old baby at an auction in Arizona."

The airplane wasn't recognizable to Frank, not as a Cessna or a Boeing 707. Matt explained that it *was* a 707, but he had got it cheap because it was customized.

"Let's get on board," Matt said. "It's a long flight to Caracas, and I heard there might be a doozy of a storm down there later."

Frank and Joe got busy stowing their gear. Everybody buckled up. Matt fired up the engines and waited for clearance from the control tower to take off.

The radio crackled to life, announcing their clearance. The takeoff was smooth, and the plane reached cruising altitude at about twenty thousand feet.

"Gentlemen," Matt announced cheerfully over the drone of the engines, "I've turned off the seat belt sign. Relax and I'll serve you a little lunch." Matt hauled a canvas tote bag into the aisle. It was filled with sandwiches made with thick slices of Italian bread.

"Excellent!" Joe crowed, lunging for the bag. "You saved my life."

"There's a great little bakery a few blocks from Maddie's place," Matt said. "I bought the bread this morning, fresh out of the oven."

"How did the plane check out this morning?" Oren asked, furrowing his brow. "Did it appear to be secure?" Matt nodded and took a bite of his sandwich.

Frank turned to Oren. "Are you worried about sabotage?" he asked the professor.

"Sabotage?" Matt turned around. "What's this about sabotage?"

Joe and Frank told them about the events of the night before. Matt and Sogyal listened with interest.

"Oren's right to be worried," Matt said.

"Relax," John said. "Oren's just a mother hen about airplanes. His people believe that if man were meant to fly, he would have been born with wings."

Joe was still worried.

"Carlos Cruz must have contacts in North America," Frank said. "That steamer trunk trick sure seemed like a terrorist tactic."

John shook his head. "How would Cruz know what we're up to? He'd have to have spies even in jail with Ed."

"Well, somebody sure followed me to the edge of that subway platform and pushed me," Joe chimed in. He popped the last bite of sandwich in his mouth. "Besides, anyone who knew Ed's connection with The People could have been keeping track of you guys. Maybe they figured you'd try to help him."

"Just for the record, Carlos and his Red Shirts have fans all over the world," Oren said. "I think we should try to take naps so we'll be able to face whatever we get to South America."

Everybody rested for a while. John even fell asleep and started snoring lightly.

Frank turned to Sogyal, noticing his eyes were open, and broke the silence. "I've been meaning to ask you. What do you know about Harvey Brinkman?" he asked. "We ran into him downtown yesterday. He said he was trying to get in to see Ed."

"Ah, Brinkman," Sogyal said with a sigh. "He's a fast talker, an opportunist."

"At the party you mentioned that he once worked for O'Neill," Joe said to Oren.

"Yeah," Oren replied. "That was around the time Maddie staged the demonstration to inform the world that O'Neill was helping burn down the rain forest. Harvey came up with an ad campaign to try to convince people O'Neill was a great, rugged conservationist like Teddy Roosevelt."

"And now he's an importer?" Joe asked.

"That's right," Oren said. "He's what you'd call a jack-of-all-trades, I guess." Catching Joe's train of thought, he added, "But he has nothing against Ed, as far as I know. And he idolizes Roger O'Neill."

The combination of a full stomach and the drone of the plane's engine lulled Joe to sleep a few minutes later. He woke up in about four hours to the twinkling lights of a city below.

"Caracas," Frank told him.

"Let me be your tour guide," Matt said, beginning a steep descent. "If you look out the cabin window, you may catch a glimpse of El Avila—a huge mountain peak that looms over Caracas. Too bad it's so overcast—you'd see that we're actually flying through the Andes to land in Caracas."

"Cool," Joe said, excited to be landing in South America at sunset.

"Cool indeed," Matt said. "You see, Caracas is nestled in a valley in the most northern cordillera, or mountain range, of the Andes. Picture a long, curving spine, and we're landing somewhere in the neck." He contacted the control tower.

"You're number three for landing," said an air traffic controller in the tower. "The wind is two-seven-zero at fifteen knots, with gusts to twenty-five. The altimeter is three-zero-zero-two."

Suddenly Matt turned white. "We've got a problem, folks," he said in a tense voice. The plane had just started veering crazily to the left. He worked the controls. The tower started directing him again.

"I've got an indicator problem here, tower," Matt said. "Leave me alone for a minute." The plane veered even more sharply to the left. Matt fought for control. Joe could see that sweat was pouring into Matt's eyes, blinding him. He blotted his eyes with his forearm and tried to control the plane. It spun even more wildly.

"Tower," Matt said. "I've got hydraulic failure, split flaps, and marginal controls. I need immediate clearance to land."

"Split flaps? What's going on?" Joe asked sharply.

"The flaps on the wings that steer the plane," Oren said. "One of them's stuck." He craned his head to peer out the window. "Now it looks like the other one's stuck, too. Plus, the controls don't work." Fear filled his eyes.

"Come on, Matt," Frank called from the back, a slight tremor in his voice. "Get us out of this."

"Roger," the tower replied. The voice directed Matt to an abandoned parallel runway. "You're clear to land, seven-oh-seven, come straight in. We've got foam and fire trucks standing by. Good luck, amigo."

"Thanks, amigo," Matt said. "Please don't let us crash in the Andes," he added prayerfully.

"Okay, everybody," Matt said in a voice that was straining to be normal. "Let's brace for a crash. Put your pillow in your lap and bury your face in it. Now."

The ground was rising up fast to meet them. Joe could see fire trucks and people running around at the end of the runway, as small as toys. Joe shut his eyes and obeyed Matt's orders.

Moments later the 707 hit the runway at a forty-five-degree angle. Joe felt as if he had been pounded down through the floor of the plane. He didn't even know if he was dead or alive at first, but he picked up his head and discovered he was okay. It was dark, and bags and leftover sandwiches flew everywhere. The cabin was a wind tunnel now, tearing up pieces of itself and spitting them out, screeching like some demonic animal. Joe got on his knees and crawled toward the emergency exit over the wing, counting seat backs because he knew he and Frank were four seats from the exit.

"Frank," he tried to call, but it came out in a rasp. The cabin was filling with smoke. He heard someone coughing up ahead, maybe John. Suddenly there was a blast of fresh air and light.

"Hurry," Oren called.

Joe crawled to the spot and tumbled out, gasping in great lungfuls of air. He scrambled over the wing, and fell down onto the hard runway. Unseen arms lifted him and helped him run. He heard a deep boom, followed by a roar. The dusky dark turned orange. He knew the plane had exploded.

Chapter

6

JOE WHIRLED AROUND, covering his face with one arm. Twisted hunks of metal were strewn everywhere. The runway was being covered with foam, to help contain a fuel fire.

In the distance he saw Oren, John, and Sogyal kneeling over a prone figure. A rescue crew was running toward them. Joe tried to run, too, but he felt a sharp pain in his ankle. He had twisted it when he jumped from the plane.

Frank, Joe thought, panic-stricken as he approached the figure on the ground. Please let him be okay—

"It's Matt," Sogyal said when Joe was in earshot. "His leg's cut badly in several places, and there may be internal injuries. But I think he'll be okay."

"Then where's Frank?" Joe glanced around anxiously for his brother as the rescue team hoisted Matt onto a gurney. A ball of fear formed in Joe's stomach. Oren and John walked over to him. They were covered with cuts and had the same grave question in their eyes. All at once Oren's eyes lit up.

"Look behind you, Joe," Walker said.

Frank loped straight out of the burning wreckage. His lopsided grin was dazzlingly white because he was completely covered with soot. From a distance he looked like a mirage, his outline shimmering against the wall of heat from the fire.

"Yo," he called. "I'm glad you guys didn't think about leaving without me." Though he was trying to be jovial, Joe could see that Frank was trembling.

"You are one lucky person," John said with relief. "Next time don't cut it so close."

"I was thrown clear," Frank said. "I just had farther to walk than you guys. And, John, I don't plan on there being a next time!"

The Venezuelan police and security clustered around Matt. The senior officer read back each statement Matt made. Then Matt was loaded into an ambulance. Sogyal climbed in after him, promising Oren to look after the pilot until he recovered.

"I wish you were coming with us," Joe said.

"So do I," Sogyal replied. "But we'll keep in

touch. Matt could be out of the hospital in a day or two."

After the ambulance drove away, there was more discussion with the police and a couple of radio calls to confirm that Frank, Joe, Oren, and John had indeed arranged to stay at the home of Elena Vargas, a prominent anthropologist. They got a curt nod from the senior officer on the scene. Vargas had vouched for them. They could go.

The police escorted them through customs and out to the front of the airport. Frank didn't think they were liked or trusted, and he tried to convince himself that was good—the police wouldn't interfere.

Outside the airport it seemed to Frank that a hundred cabdrivers clamored for their business. Oren haggled with the driver of a reasonably safe-looking old junker, and finally the group set off. The taxi merged onto a wide highway and passed into a long tunnel through a mountain.

They emerged from the tunnel into slow-motion chaos. The skyscrapers of Caracas glimmered ahead, but the cab was trapped in a stagnant sea of cars. It was rush hour, but nobody was rushing anywhere. Mercedes, jalopies, and trucks were locked together head to tail, horns blasting. The taxi driver pounded on the wheel, shouting in Spanish.

"The controls were stuck, and the landing flaps

split," John said angrily. "When I find out who's responsible for this, I swear I'll make them pay."

"I'm just grateful we all survived," Oren remarked, sinking low in his seat. Frank watched him as he gazed out the window. A moment later Oren asked, "Don't you wonder what the Yanomama think when they come out of the jungle for the first time and see this?"

After an eternity the cab started moving again, climbing mountainside northwest of the city. The air was cooler, and the houses and condos were spacious and attractive.

The cab pulled up in front of a sparkling white ranch house. A small, middle-aged woman was waiting for them in the doorway.

"Thank heavens you're all right," she said, hugging Oren.

"Guys, this is Elena Vargas," Oren said. "She's one of the best anthropologists around."

"Next to Oren Walker!" Elena laughed. She ushered them all inside. Frank saw that it was a small house but cool and tidy. The dining room table was spread with a light supper of fruit, cold chicken, rice, and beans.

"This is the best sight I've seen all day," Frank said, his stomach growling.

Joe agreed. "Let's wash up and eat."

When they were showered and fed—and dressed in tropical clothes provided by Elena, which more or less fit them—Frank, Joe, and John listened to Oren and Elena talk about the beauties and dangers of the rain forest. They learned that Oren had been in the forest twice before.

"Really, the destruction is not so bad in Venezuela yet," Elena said. "It's worse in Brazil, where vast areas of ravaged forest have become desert."

"But now," Oren said, "I've heard that gold speculators are starting to move into Yanomama territory on the Brazil-Venezuela border. The damage they can do with their mines is incredible."

"Elena, do you think the Yanomama could have kidnapped Roger O'Neill?" Joe asked.

Frank watched Oren glare at Joe.

"It's possible the Yanomama did do it," said Elena. "I can't say I'd blame them. Here, they've lived in perfect harmony with the forests for a millennium. And if O'Neill had been planning to level parts of it—no one could protect them."

"I don't buy it," John objected. "Who sabotaged the plane? Who pushed Joe onto the subway tracks in New York? It can't be the Yanomama, even if they do have the best motive."

"Perhaps they had help," Elena said.

"You mean Maddie?" Oren asked, staring at Elena with slow-dawning shock.

"No, Oren, for the record I don't think it was Maddie," Elena said. "Though we both know she's the kind of woman who gets impatient. Let me explain what I've been able to find out. After I heard that O'Neill had been kidnapped and that Ed was accused of the crime, I tried to get a look at O'Neill's car myself. The police wouldn't let me see the car nor would they discuss the case with me. Without the cooperation of the police and with no leads, trying to hunt down the kidnapper is hopeless."

"Then what are we doing here?" Frank asked, disappointed.

"That remains to be seen," Elena told him curtly. She turned back to the rest of the group. "I have heard a strange rumor," she continued. "A native friend of mine tells me that a man resembling O'Neill has been spotted in the forest. It's possible that the kidnappers took him there. If that's true, we're left with several possible suspects: Carlos Cruz, the Da Silva brothers, who head a very powerful cattle-raising clan here, and, as much as I hate to admit it, Maddie."

"So our only chance of catching them is to find O'Neill in the forest!" Frank exclaimed.

"The forest?" Oren frowned. "I was hoping we wouldn't have to go in there. John and I aren't young anymore. A trek could prove fatal."

"Don't start looking for a nursing home just yet, Oren," John said, tossing his ponytail over his shoulder. "We have to find O'Neill. I'm in."

"We'd be putting Frank and Joe in grave danger, John," Oren protested.

"It won't be the first time," Joe said simply.

"Before you go into the forest, I know a bush pilot who can take you to Father Juan's mission," Elena said. "You may remember it. It's the last stop in the 'civilized world'—a place to catch boats and guides upriver. You could fly there tomorrow at dawn."

"You're an angel, Elena," John said. "But we can't go into the rain forest without supplies."

"Follow me," Elena said with a smile. She led the group to a storage room, where Frank saw sleeping bags, a portable radio set, a bag marked with a red cross for medicine, and piles of men's tropic-weight clothes.

Elena pointed to three separate duffel bags. "These contain trade goods for the Yanomama—machetes, clothes, and beaded ankle bands. Give them these and they'll welcome you with open arms."

"How did you get all of this stuff together so fast?" Oren asked.

"A lot of it was already together," Elena said. "I keep my equipment and trade goods packed. As for the men's clothes, I dropped in on some of my neighbors while you were driving over. They were glad to help. And now," she added with a wide smile for the Hardys, "I'd recommend turning in. You have a long day tomorrow."

At dawn the next day Elena drove the group to La Carlota, a private airstrip in downtown Caracas. The warm early morning air seemed fresh to Frank as he breathed it in through the open window. He could almost imagine what this area had been like before there were cars.

"What about Sogyal?" he asked Oren. "How will he know what happened to us?"

"Elena will call the hospital as soon as she returns home," Joe told him from the front seat. "After Matt's discharged from the hospital, he and Sogyal can stay with her."

Frank nodded, leaning back in his seat again. Somehow, he knew that with Elena Vargas taking care of them, Matt and Sogyal would be perfectly safe.

"All right, everybody, start unloading," Elena said as she parked her station wagon within sight of the charter plane.

The aircraft was a shock to Frank. It was a Convair Allison 580, an old American propeller plane that looked as if it should have been retired with Eisenhower. It stood at one end of the airstrip among military planes and sleek Learjets and Cessnas. It was a fat white duck among swans. "It's a classic." Elena laughed. "It's made the journey up the Orinoco many times."

"I bet," Joe said. "Maybe a million times."

The pilot, a tall young man with a bright smile, ushered them on board immediately. There was plenty of room for their gear, even for the aluminum boat and outboard motor that Elena had provided.

"Just look at all the military planes and jeeps!" Elena exclaimed. She was going to the mission with them and then returning home. "Just a few weeks ago there was a rebel strike on the capital. The newspapers claim it was the work of Carlos Cruz."

"Somehow, that doesn't surprise me," Frank said.

Elena nodded. "For seven years Cruz has been attacking this country," she told Frank. "When the authorities get too close, he hides out in the jungle. Whatever you do, avoid that man."

Not long after takeoff, Frank saw the rain forest stretching out like a green carpet to the horizon. A mist hung over the trees, and the Orinoco River sliced through the green paradise like a silver ribbon.

"If anybody has heard anything about Yanomama involvement in the kidnapping, it will be Father Juan," Elena said. "The few Yanomama who visit the white man's world always pass by Ocamo on their way downriver in their dugouts."

"Señora Vargas," the pilot interrupted, "I can't contact the mission on the radio."

Frank felt the plane begin to descend. He glanced out of his window. All he could see was miles of endless forest.

"That's odd," Elena said. "I spoke to Father Juan last night. He's expecting us." She looked at Frank and Joe. "Radios are our lifeline out here, but no machines are infallible in the jungle."

Frank kept his vigil at the window until he spotted the runway. He breathed a sigh of relief when the pilot made a smooth landing. He had had all the airborne excitement he could stand for the rest of his life. He noticed that the runway was deserted.

"I wonder where Father Juan is," Elena said, sounding even more alarmed. The pilot talked in rapid Spanish to Elena as they taxied to a stop. For a few moments Elena argued with him, but it seemed to Frank that the pilot had won the dispute.

"He said it looks like rain," Elena said, turning to the Hardys in exasperation. "I'm sorry, but we must take off immediately. We can't risk getting caught in a storm in this old plane. I will stay in touch by radio."

Quickly Oren, John, and the Hardys unloaded their gear from the plane. Frank watched the Convair wheel around and take off. Suddenly the little group was alone in the forest, enormous trees and thick, hanging vines pressing in on every side. Wiping his forehead with his sleeve, Frank watched the plane until it became a speck in the distance.

"It feels like we're in the middle of nowhere," Frank said, raising his eyes to the canopy of tree-tops high above them.

"Not exactly," Joe said.

Frank lowered his eyes and looked around him. Young men in red shirts were stepping out from among the trees, walking toward them from every direction. Each one had a rifle. None of them was smiling.

"Uh, Frank," Joe muttered, his eyes never leaving the menacing crowd, "tell me those shirts aren't red. Please."

"They sure don't look friendly," John whispered. "I've got a bad feeling about this."

"Hands above your heads," one of the young men snapped in heavily accented English. "Follow me and nobody talks."

Chapter

7

FRANK AND THE OTHERS were marched single file toward the mission compound, which was set in a small clearing in the forest. The compound consisted of several cinder-block buildings and a small wooden church. Frank noticed there were no people, other than Cruz's men posted along the border.

Every few steps Frank was jabbed in the ribs by one of the dozens of rifle barrels trained on him. Frank watched the back of Joe's head, willing him not to lose his cool. Outside the church they were frisked for weapons and then motioned inside.

"What are you Americans doing in my country?" Frank heard the man's growl before he could make out the figure seated at the front of the cool, dark chapel. The man was stocky and bearded, dressed in a red shirt and baggy trousers tucked into heavy boots. Frank guessed he was in his early forties. "Did the government send you to spy on me?"

Carlos Cruz! Frank recognized the man's face from the photographs in the newspaper clippings at Maddie's apartment. Frank turned from Joe to Oren to John for a clue as to how to answer, then went ahead himself. "We're looking for the priest who runs this mission," he said. "Where is he?"

Carlos shrugged. "This place was deserted when we arrived here last night," he snarled. Frank was struck by how well he spoke English. "What do you want with Father Juan?"

"We're hoping he can help us find a man who was kidnapped in Caracas," Frank said bravely. "His name is Roger O'Neill."

Carlos grimaced. "O'Neill would make burgers out of human beings if he could get away with it. In Brazil, starving peasants cleared the forest for nothing so ranchers could get rich grazing cattle for O'Neill. Here, I do not allow such men to exploit our people."

"An innocent man is in jail, accused of kidnapping O'Neill," Joe said. "We're here to prove he didn't do it."

"Ah, yes. Eduardo, the Yanomama boy wonder," Carlos sneered. "Ed worries about trees when thousands of people are starving. I would destroy the whole forest to save one hungry Venezuelan."

"Then you're no better than O'Neill," Joe snapped.

Carlos nodded at the young men who had led Frank and the others in. "Take them away," he commanded. "They're too stupid to understand."

The guards stepped up and tied Oren's, John's, and the Hardys' wrists with thick, coarse rope. Then the men pushed their captives out of the chapel, leading them to a small, thatched building on stilts on the outer edge of the compound. Inside the building the guards bound their prisoners' ankles with the same rough rope and ordered them, with gestures and shouts in a foreign language, to lie down on the mats on the floor. Just as the guards left, a clap of thunder split the air, and a torrent of rain came pouring down.

What next? Frank wondered. It was hot and clammy inside the tiny hut. With his hands tied, he couldn't bat the insects away or keep the sweat out of his eyes.

"We've got to get out of these ropes," Joe whispered to the others as soon as the guards had left. "Frank, if I get over to you, you can work on my wrists." Joe wriggled over to his brother. Back to back, they tried to pick at the tight knots in the rope.

"Forget it, Joe," Frank said at last. "These guys know how to tie a knot."

"I say we try to sleep until it's cooler," Oren

suggested. "There's nothing we can do in the meantime."

"Where are we?" Joe asked. Frank could hear the frustration in his brother's voice. "I'm not even sure what's going on."

"Well, for one thing, we've stumbled onto Cruz's secret camp," Frank pointed out. "He won't let us go if he thinks we'll report his location to the authorities. My guess now is that he has something to do with the kidnapping after all. You heard what he said about O'Neill, and he seems preoccupied with something."

John spoke up. "For all we know, he may have killed Father Juan. But Oren's right. Sleep is a good defense. We need to conserve our energy."

The four wriggled in opposite directions, trying to find cool spots. Frank was near the door. Exhausted by the events of the past two days, he fell asleep almost immediately to the pounding of the heavy rain. He woke up when he felt a strange tickling moving across his chest. "What's that?" he cried, waking the others instantly.

"Army ants!" Oren hissed. "Don't move. Those things eat crocodiles."

Frank obeyed, barely breathing as he watched the ants march over his chest. There were thousands of them, it seemed—each nearly two inches long. Outside, rain poured down. A flash of lightning lit up the faces of Oren, John, and Joe, as they stared at Frank's chest with still, worried expressions.

After an hour that passed like a lifetime, the last ants had marched over Frank, into the center of the room, and out a hole in the corner of the building.

"Did you feel like a giant picnic basket?" Joe asked, relief sounding in his voice.

"They're blind, you know," Oren said. "And direct sunlight kills them."

"Right," John said, "but blindness doesn't stop them. They can cross rivers by rolling themselves up into a ball and floating to the other side. And when they bite into a piece of meat, they never let go. In Africa, some people use army ant heads to hold wounds closed, like stitches."

"Very interesting," Joe replied. "We'll have to remember that next time they take a stroll across my brother's chest."

Just then Frank heard a woman's voice, clearly American, arguing with Carlos. The voices drew closer. Frank turned to Oren and saw the concern on the man's face.

"Oren!" John said. "Do you think that's—"

"Maddie Hatfield," Oren muttered. "Shh! Let's listen."

Quietly Frank and the others wriggled closer to the door so they could hear better over the noise of the rain.

"We had a deal!" Frank heard the woman shout in a flat, midwestern accent.

"Yes, you agreed to teach us the chemical

properties of rain forest plants," Carlos Cruz replied. "You have yet to deliver."

"I won't show you how to make curare or other poisons," Maddie said. "We agreed to stop at tranquilizers."

"Curare?" Frank whispered. Maddie knew how to make curare. She could have made it to frame Ed. Frank saw by the others' expressions that they were thinking the same thing.

Maddie continued. "You have no right to hold those guys here. They've done nothing to you. And I'm certainly not going to help you kill them."

"Maddie, we went to school together," Carlos said. "We were good friends back then. That is why I could never bring myself to harm you. But these friends of yours are strangers and possibly spies."

"They're here to find evidence to clear Ed," Maddie pleaded. "I'm sure of it. They came to see Father Juan. Let them go, Carlos."

"They have no business being around here," Carlos said. "I can't let you see them, and I won't let them go." The pair walked off, still arguing despite the rain.

"They must have thought we were asleep," Frank whispered. "Thank you, army ants."

"There's a use for everything," John said— only he wasn't smiling.

Frank must have dozed off, because when he woke the rain had stopped. His thirst was all but unbearable. A moment later Maddie Hatfield appeared in the doorway carrying a jug of water and four tin cups.

"Hello, Maddie," Oren said softly, struggling to sit up.

"I'm sorry about this, Oren, John," Maddie said, setting the water down and pulling a knife from a sheath on her belt.

"Not half as sorry as we are," John admonished.

She cut them free and told them to drink quickly. Frank watched Maddie, who was sitting propped up against the back wall of the little hut. She appeared to be in her late thirties, tall and tanned, with a mane of honey-colored hair. It was hard to make out details in the dim light, but she seemed to have a kind, intelligent face. Frank had to admit that Maddie Hatfield didn't look like an evil kidnapper.

"There's food," she said. "It's in the boat. We have to hurry now, while the camp is resting and Carlos is in a meeting."

"What's going on, Maddie?" Oren said. "We heard you mention Ed. Did you know he's in prison—"

"Carlos told me," Maddie said. "Look, I know how weird this looks, my being in Carlos's camp."

"It does look weird," John snapped. "Especially since you were talking to Cruz about curare

69

and tranquilizers. Did you know the kidnappers left curare in O'Neill's car."

Maddie stared at John incredulously. "Are you accusing me of being involved in O'Neill's disappearance? I thought you knew me better than that, John. I would never do anything to hurt Ed." She stared hard at him before continuing. "Come on—before we get stopped."

"Let's go," Joe said, getting up. "I don't know what's going on, but I don't want to spend another minute here." The others agreed and stole silently through the area.

The compound was deserted in the heat of the afternoon. Down at the small dock at the river's edge, a small, bow-legged native waited in a dugout canoe with an eight-horsepower motor. He stood about five feet tall, with black hair that fell in bangs to his alert black eyes. A black leather armband with a brilliant yellow parrot feather stuck in it contrasted with his nut brown skin. Besides the armband, he wore nothing but a red loincloth.

When the man saw Maddie, he broke into a wide grin, revealing a gold front tooth. He studied Frank, Joe, and the others, but his eyes returned to Maddie.

"Where are we going?" Joe asked in a low voice.

"This man is from Ed's tribe," Maddie replied. "He'll take you to Ed's father's village. Maybe you can learn more about O'Neill there. In any case, you'll be safe from Cruz."

Frank extended his hand to the Yanomama, who just stared at it curiously.

"What's your name?" Joe asked slowly.

"He cannot tell you that," Maddie interjected. "It's considered taboo in the Yanomama culture. But I trust him."

"I'll just call him Gold Tooth then," Joe said.

Frank noticed that the boat was crammed with the equipment Elena had packed for them with the addition of the first-aid kit and the radio transmitter they had brought on the plane. Maddie took a revolver out of her backpack and handed it to Oren. He pushed it roughly away.

"Take it," she said. "It might save your life."

"I'll take it," John said firmly, snatching the gun from Maddie's hand. "Will you be all right, Maddie?"

"Carlos won't hurt me. I have too much to teach him. He needs me."

After the group had climbed into the boat and pushed off, they paddled upriver. At first Frank thought that the dense, green jungle lining the river was beautiful but familiar, a bit like Florida. As he studied it more closely, he realized that the bushes and flowers and trees passing by were incredible in their variety—few were anything he had seen before.

After a while the Yanomama started the motor, and John took over the steering. Frank and Joe stretched out on the equipment, happy to lie back and take in the scenery.

"Am I glad to be out of there," Joe said.

"We have Maddie Hatfield to thank for that," Oren said.

Frank nodded. "I'll thank her for that, but I believe she may still be mixed up in the kidnapping somehow."

Joe couldn't believe his brother. "Then why would she help us escape?"

"Frank may be right, Joe," John said. "If Maddie is keeping company with a man like Carlos Cruz, something isn't right. Maybe they worked together to orchestrate the kidnapping."

Oren frowned. "That doesn't sit right with me. Maddie would never frame Ed. I don't believe it."

Frank shrugged. "Maybe we'll find some answers in Ed's village. I hope Ed's father will tell us if any Yanomama were involved in the kidnapping."

"If they were involved, I'm not sure how happy they're going to be, having us snoop around," Joe said. "But Ed's father has to be interested in getting his son out of jail. Think of how Dad would feel."

His words were drowned out by a rushing sound from up ahead.

"What's that?" Frank asked, sitting up.

"If I remember correctly," Oren said, "we should be coming to the Guajaribo Rapids. It's lucky we—" His words were interrupted by the sound of the engine sputtering and dying. As Frank watched tensely, John threw back the engine cover.

"Somebody's tampered with the fitting!" John yelled over the sound of the rushing water. "We've been leaking oil."

"And here come the rapids!" Joe shouted.

An instant later the boat slammed into the rapids broadside. Joe saw that Frank was about to pitch overboard, and he quickly grabbed him by the back of the shirt. He could see Oren and John grab oars and begin to paddle to turn the boat around before they hit a drop-off and a new set of rapids. Gold Tooth sat in the bow of the boat, smiling at the water.

"Here, Joe!" Frank called out. He handed a pair of oars to his brother.

Before Joe could grab them, though, the boat, caught in a fierce current, swung around a curve.

"Hang on, Joe!" he heard Frank shout as he lurched violently to the side of the boat.

The next thing Joe knew, he was airborne and sailing into the swirling white water, which buried him like an avalanche and dragged him under.

Chapter

8

JOE TUMBLED until he didn't know up from down. When the water quieted, he fought his way up—what he hoped was up—like a wild animal. Just when he thought his lungs would burst, he saw blue sky above him. In a second he was up and out of the water, gasping for air. Frank swam up to him then, looped an arm around his chest, and pulled him toward a rocky island in the middle of the river.

"Hang on," Frank panted. "It gets shallow real quick." In a few strokes Frank stood up and waded. Joe followed on shaky legs. Oren and John waved from the tiny island. The Yanomama sat to one side. Frank hauled himself onto the shore.

"Whew, I think you've put on a few pounds, little brother," Frank said.

"I soaked up a few gallons of water," Joe replied.

"Catch your breath," Oren said. "We have some more swimming to do." Frank noticed that Oren and John had piled up the equipment they had managed to save—an oar, the medical supplies, a small duffel bag full of machetes and fishing line that were to be traded with the Yanomama. The radio was gone. Gold Tooth stared straight ahead, hugging his knees with his arms.

"What's his story?" Joe asked. The Yanomama's round face had turned to stone.

"He may have sabotaged the engine," John said. "I'm trying hard to believe that Maddie didn't tell him to do it."

"So you think she had something to do with O'Neill?" Frank asked.

"Maybe," John said. "And maybe this Yanomama helped her."

"Nothing Maddie has done adds up," Oren said, pain in his dark eyes. "But we'll have plenty of time to figure it out when we get to the riverbank."

They were past the worst of the rapids, so they distributed the equipment among them and swam downstream side by side. John and Oren tied the Yanomama's wrists to the oar and pulled him along. They were careful to keep his head above water.

"When we find a translator, I want to interrogate this guy," John explained. "Meanwhile, I don't want him to get away. We're going to have to keep him under wraps until we find Ed's tribe."

A few minutes downstream they came to smooth water. Joe lay out on his back on the river's surface and ya-hooed to the sky.

"Good idea, Joe," Frank said. "You decided to let the Red Shirts know exactly where we are. Now they can come get us easier."

"Well, maybe they'll keep the piranhas away." John chuckled. He stood up and started wading to the riverbank. "I think the piranhas hang out near the shore," he called back to the others.

Joe and Frank splashed for shore and scrambled up the riverbank, watching Oren lead the captive Yanomama. Neither of them seemed concerned about piranhas.

"What you really have to watch out for are *candiru*," Oren said. "They're little catfish the size of toothpicks. They swim into ears, mouths, every opening in the body. They shoot off spines that have to be surgically removed."

Frank saw that even the Yanomama smiled at the mention of candiru, and Frank caught on that their companions were teasing them. There probably were piranhas and candiru here in the forest—but Frank guessed that they weren't an ever-present danger. On the other hand, Frank thought as he slapped his arm, the swarms of biting gnats, so tiny they were almost invisible, were a problem.

"Remind me never to complain about the mosquitoes in Bayport again," Joe said to Frank, regretting opening his mouth as he inhaled a mouthful of the gnats.

Frank didn't know which was worse—the gnats, or his soggy clothes. The rain had started again, though not as heavily as before, and he felt as if he would never be dry again.

Frank followed the others into the edge of the forest. He and Joe helped Oren tie Gold Tooth in a tree with fishing line. Joe wrapped his ankles in leaves so the line wouldn't cut them.

"No smile of thanks?" Joe asked the Yanomama. "If this guy doesn't show us the way to Ed's village, we're lost. We can't go back the way we came." Frank could see his brother was beginning to feel uneasy.

"He probably thought he could get away from us in the water," Oren said. "But I think he still wants to go home. He might not be happy about leading us, but he knows we can't sit here forever. All we can do is dig in and wait till he's had enough of sitting."

The rain stopped and what seemed like hours passed, and Joe was beginning to think that Gold Tooth would never get tired of sitting. "I guess people have a different attitude about time in the rain forest," he said to Frank as he stared at the Yanomama, who calmly returned his stare. "After all, not much seems to change here."

Joe found some chores to pass the time. Oren had showed the Hardys how to dig a shallow hearth with machetes. They had foraged for dry wood, and thanks to some waterproof matches in the medical supply pack, they now had a small fire.

There were fewer gnats here, farther from the riverbank, Joe noted gratefully, but they kept biting. They flew into eyes and ears and mouths, and even though they didn't shoot spines, their bites were like tiny bee stings. They seemed to like Joe best. Within a couple of hours his back was a mass of welts. Oren got mud from the riverbank and mixed it with cortisone lotion to soothe the burning.

The Yanomama didn't pay attention to any of the goings-on.

"Look at him," Joe said, growing even more impatient. "Even the bugs don't bite him."

"They bite him," Oren said. "He's just not going to show us it bothers him."

"Just like he's not going to show us that he understands every word we're saying," John said.

"He doesn't understand every word," Oren said, watching the Yanomama. "But his gold tooth tells us he's spent time out of the forest. He could well understand key English words."

"Yeah," John chimed in. "Like, 'kill the motor.'"

"Or maybe, 'Kill the men in the boat,'" Joe added.

"No!" the Yanomama yelled, struggling against the fishing line. "No kill! No kill!"

"We're not going to kill you," John said. He turned to the others. "We'll all starve if we sit here too long. Let's fish for our dinner."

Oren got fishing line and hooks from the duffel bag and handed them to Frank and Joe.

"What are we going to use for bait?" Joe asked.

"How about this?" John pulled a half-eaten roll of cherry LifeSavers from his pocket. "The fish might like the color," he said with a grin.

After fishing for an hour, John, Frank, and Joe came back with a couple of real piranhas. Oren, who had stayed behind, used his machete to hack together a crude rotisserie.

"Gold Tooth still hasn't spoken," Oren said. "We have to feed him, anyway." The piranha was tough, bony, and bland. John tried to boil water to drink in a shallow tray he found in a medical kit, but it boiled over and left almost nothing.

"I think we can risk drinking the river water," Oren said. "Just remember to take your antimalaria tablets."

Night fell, turning the dim forest utterly dark in moments. "That's because we're near the equator," Frank told Joe. "Day and night are each twelve hours long, with no long sunsets or dawns."

Still hungry, the men took off their wet shoes and clothes and hung them to dry on the bushes. They formed a sleeping circle around the tiny fire. Oren untied the Yanomama and allowed him to lie down. Then he tied his hands and wrists together and gave him a long, deep drink of water.

Joe fell asleep listening to the sounds of the forest. He wondered about Roger O'Neill. Where was he? What had he been up to before he was kidnapped? His last thought before falling asleep was of Maddie Hatfield. Was she really responsible for the motor conking out? Could she have been capable of such an act? And if she and Carlos Cruz had kidnapped O'Neill, where were they hiding him?

Sometime in the middle of the night Joe woke because of a stinging sensation on his leg. He looked down to see something wet and dark lying across his foot and ankle. He sat up with a jerk in time to see it flutter off.

"Bats!" he screamed. "Vampire bats!" Instantly Joe was up, yowling with pain and hopping toward the river by the moonlight.

"Sit down," Oren commanded. Joe felt hands pushing him down. "Vampire bats inject an anticoagulant that can make the blood trickle out for hours. The more you jump around, the more you're going to bleed. Don't worry. You'll be all right."

Everybody was up. "Don't listen to him, Joe," John kidded. "By this time tomorrow night, you'll be sprouting fangs and turning into a bat yourself."

"What'll really kill him," Frank added, "is not being able to see his reflection in the mirror."

"Very funny, guys," Joe complained. "That was the lousiest wake-up call I've ever gotten."

Joe glanced over to where Gold Tooth had been sleeping. "The Yanomama!" Joe shouted. "He's gone." He knelt down and picked up a handful of melted fishing line, as frizzled as burned hair. A smoldering log from the fire lay nearby. "It looks like he burned through the line on his ankles. The leaves I wrapped around his skin kept him from getting burned."

"Great!" Oren said, disgusted. "Now how are we going to find Ed's village?"

"We'll just have to hunt it down ourselves," Joe declared. Embarrassed over the bat incident, he hoped he sounded brave and certain. "All we have to do is wait for daylight and follow the river."

Oren nodded. "That makes sense. It's likely that the village is near the river, so the Yanomama can travel," Oren replied.

Just then Joe heard the rumbling of a motorboat in the night air. Motioning to the others, he crept to the river's edge in time to see Maddie Hatfield cruising upstream in a boat filled with Carlos's rebels.

"Do you think they're gathering plants?" Joe asked.

As Maddie's boat chugged out of sight, Oren was obviously upset. "Maybe we should have yelled at her. She could lead us to Ed's village," he said.

"We need a guide," John told him. "The forest is dangerous, but until we find out what side Maddie is on, we have to consider her even more dangerous."

Joe glanced over at Oren. The older man acted depressed. "John's right," Oren finally admitted, and lumbered back toward the fire.

The foursome agreed to get more sleep before starting out on their journey. Joe found it hard to sleep with the strange screams and animal chatter filling the jungle.

"I thought nature was supposed to be peaceful," he remarked.

"Nature's anything *but* peaceful," Oren scoffed in the darkness. "This is not an easy place to stay alive, even as full of life as it is."

Joe shuddered lightly. Then, lost in his thoughts, he fell asleep. Near dawn he woke up—or dreamed he woke up, he wasn't sure. A moment later he heard something rattling the bush in front of him. Sitting up, Joe stared at the bush, a sudden chill racing up his spine. He tried to call out to the others, but no words would come.

Then Joe heard a twig break, and a shadow emerged from the bush.

"What—" Joe muttered, staring straight ahead. Staring back at him were the flashing green eyes of a jaguar.

Chapter

9

"FRANK," JOE WHISPERED, afraid to move. "Anybody, please. Wake up."

The jaguar seemed to be studying him; its bright eyes looked intelligent but wild. Joe watched, paralyzed, as the jaguar coiled back on his haunches to lunge. He stopped there, however, and snaked off backward through the underbrush. By the time Frank and the others woke up, the animal had vanished.

"What's up, Joe?" Frank asked. He walked over to Joe and peered into his face. "You look like you saw a ghost."

"A jaguar," Joe said. "Maybe a jaguar ghost. It was standing over there near that bush."

"When?" Oren asked, sitting up groggily.

"Just now," Joe said. "It backed up and disappeared."

Joe took a deep breath and walked slowly in the direction of the bush where the jaguar had stood. He thought there had to be a sign that it had been there—a bit of fur, a broken twig. There was nothing. Oren and John joined him, and they fanned out from the spot, to search for the jaguar. It was quite light, and the heat was rising. After a few minutes they gave up.

"I think you dreamed this jaguar, Joe," Frank said. "An animal that big has to bend a twig or leave droppings somewhere."

Oren laughed his agreement.

"Hey, I found something even more interesting," John called, pulling an object out of the ashes of their campfire.

Joe took the object from him. It was a half-melted pair of horn-rimmed glasses. The lenses were cracked and stained with something brown. Joe realized with a shock that it could be blood.

"I helped dig the pit for the fire," Joe said. "There was nothing there."

"I know," John replied. "It's totally weird."

"That's not all that's weird," Frank said. "One of our duffel bags is missing. The one with the trade goods for the Yanomama," he added, inspecting the contents of the single remaining bag. "The machetes and fishing gear are gone. So is the oar."

"Well," Joe said, setting the shattered glasses

on one of the rocks they'd used to ring the fire pit. "It looks like our friendly guide left us something to remember him by. These have to be Roger O'Neill's," Joe said. "He was wearing glasses just like these in the newspaper picture we saw before we left New York."

"Someone else could have dropped in and left them," Frank objected. "Anyway, where could he have been carrying them. He only had on a loincloth."

"Maybe it was somebody from Carlos's camp?" John said.

"I have a hunch Carlos doesn't need a bag full of machetes and fishing line," Joe said.

"But Maddie or Carlos could have done it to frame the Yanomama," John pointed out.

"I don't believe you guys!" Joe snapped. "Maddie saved us. Why do we keep blaming her?"

"Because we don't want to believe Ed's people are guilty," John said. He shook his head. "I don't know. Maybe it's time to consider the idea that Ed hatched the whole idea for the kidnapping himself. Maybe he wasn't framed."

"Then why did he ask for our help?" Frank asked.

"We don't know for sure those are O'Neill's glasses," Oren said angrily. "And we don't know if the Yanomama are involved or not. The idea of either Ed or Maddie being implicated in this is leaving a very bitter taste in my mouth."

"We'll have to wait and hope that some of our questions will be answered at Ed's village," John said. "So now all we have to do is get there."

Everybody looked more than a little spooked.

"We may as well get moving," Frank suggested, ignoring the chattering of a monkey in the tree above. "All we're doing is following the river. How hard can it be?"

"Very hard," Oren said.

"Not counting the fact that a very angry Yanomama with a gold tooth might be stalking us," Joe added.

"Well, we should get moving," Frank said. "Let's just think of the jungle as a learning experience, like a giant terrarium."

"Right, a terrarium," Joe said. "This morning I saw a fern just like one Aunt Gertrude keeps in her terrarium."

"There you go," Frank said.

"Only it was about twenty feet tall," Joe continued. "I thought a dinosaur was going to pop out from behind it any minute."

They doused the fire, packed up their gear, and started walking, sticking as close to the river as they could bear because of the insects. Within half an hour Joe realized that no sport he had ever played at Bayport High had prepared him for trekking in the jungle.

The temperature was about a hundred degrees, but the humidity made the heat feel almost solid. It was oppressive and clung to them, adding weight to their too solid bodies. Joe felt huge and clumsy.

Under the forest canopy all was shadowy and dim. The dense, green growth covered the sky and made them feel as if they were inside a huge, green cathedral. Only every detail of the cathedral was alive, breathing, crawling, and different from every other detail.

"I feel like I'm on another planet," Joe said. "I've never even seen pictures of most of these plants."

"About ninety percent of the species on the earth live in the rain forest," Oren said.

"Yeah," Frank added. "And we're losing a couple of species of plants and animals every day as the rain forest is destroyed. The cure for cancer could be in one of these plants. And many more cures are probably still undiscovered."

"Is that what Maddie does?" Joe asked. "She distills medicines from these plants, doesn't she?"

"That's right," Oren told him.

They walked single file, each of them drenched in sweat and breathing hard. It began to rain lightly. Less than an hour out, they fell into a stream, and everything they had got soaked and full of sand. They took turns hacking at the undergrowth with the one machete they had left—the one Oren had kept beside him while he slept. The insects came at them like tiny kamikaze pilots.

"Gross!" Joe yelled, sputtering. "One just flew in my mouth."

"You really have a taste for those bugs, don't you, Joe?" John joked.

"Go ahead, laugh," Joe said to him. "That bug had a wingspan this big." Joe held his hands a foot apart. He was glad to see John kidding around again, though. The humor helped take their minds off the seriousness of their situation. If he stopped to think about how lost they were, Joe realized, he'd panic—and that would get him exactly nowhere.

"This definitely is not my idea of a good time," Frank said at last, sinking down for a rest. "Is there any chance we can stop to eat?"

"I'd rather we hiked a little farther first," Oren told him. "But you can get some fresh water from the river."

"It's over this way," John said, striking out through the trees to the right. As the others followed him, he added ruefully, "Too bad I lost my sketchbook in the plane. I would love to draw some of these scenes."

"How can such a tough guy be such a good artist?" Joe asked, catching up with him on the hacked-out trail.

"You don't have to be soft to be an artist," John said, laughing. "You just have to have passion."

"And you have plenty of that, my friend," Oren agreed from behind.

"Well, I've got plenty of passion myself," Joe said, taking the machete from John and stepping in front of him on the trail. "Passion for a long drink of water, that is. And after that, no matter what you guys say, I'm going to hack down some fruit—or roots—to eat on the way."

Joe stumbled ahead, blinded by sweat, blind to everything but the wall of plant life in front of him. He was just mopping his face with the sleeve of his shirt for the hundredth time when he ran into something that felt and smelled like rancid cotton candy. "Oh, yuck!" he yelled, causing the others to stop behind him. "It's a giant spiderweb!"

Joe tried to wipe the strands from his sweaty body, but the web clung. "I don't even want to think what the spider who made this looks like," he muttered as the others crowded up behind him.

"Huge and hairy," Frank cracked. "With iron jaws. And an insatiable taste for seventeen-year-old high school kids from Bayport."

Their laughter died in their throats. At the exact time Frank and Joe noticed that the spiderweb was dangling from a limb that seemed much too straight to be a limb. The limb seemed to grow out from a kind of mossy cave. Moving closer, Joe was able to make out what it really was.

"A helicopter!" he said. The broken rotors were covered with vines and broken tree branches. The rotors jutted up in the air. "Where did *this* come from?"

"It looks like someone tried to hide it here," Oren said. "Camouflaged it with brush."

"It couldn't have been here more than a week," John announced. "I still smell fuel on the engine."

"I can't wait to see what we find inside," Joe said.

"I'm afraid we're about to find out where these glasses came from," Frank said.

Joe took a deep breath and entered.

Chapter

10

"IT'S EMPTY," Joe said.

Frank sighed with relief as he looked around. The control panel was a jumble of colored wires and rust, and a small green bird peeked out from where the altimeter had been. The seats jutted forward, torn half out of the floor. Broken glass crunched under Frank's feet. Everything was covered with lichen and new vines, but there was no body.

"Wait a minute!" Frank crouched down in the back of the helicopter. He found a brown leather wallet along with bloodied strips of clothing. Frank opened the wallet and scanned the ID.

"This was O'Neill's wallet," he said solemnly, examining the name and photograph on a New York State driver's license. "His body could be around here somewhere. I think we'd better look for it."

Everyone nodded his agreement. A thorough search of the surrounding foliage turned up no clues and no body.

"If whoever piloted this survived the crash, he probably knows what happened to O'Neill," Oren said after they called off their search. "And since the chopper was hidden on purpose, I suspect they didn't want to share the news."

Joe studied the helicopter. "If they meant to hide this, I don't think they did a very good job."

John shrugged. "Maybe they were in a hurry. Besides, what are the chances that someone would stumble across it here in the middle of nowhere?"

Frank tucked the wallet into his pants pocket. "There's nothing more we can do," he said. "We'd better hit the trail."

They walked on for about an hour without talking. Finally they entered a lush green clearing with a tiny waterfall sliding into a beautiful blue-green stream. Orchids and tender grass bloomed all around.

"Perfect," Joe said with satisfaction. "This is where we stop for the night." Everyone agreed.

John thrilled everybody by catching a fish with his bare hands. Frank couldn't help laughing as Joe tried over and over to do the same thing, managing only to fall into the cool water like a graceless rhino.

"Some things you just have to grow up learning," John said to Joe.

Frank and Oren went out for firewood and came back with armfuls of wild plantains. They built a fire and had their first real meal in almost two days. While he ate, Frank listened to the splash of the waterfall and the whoops and cries of the birds, monkeys, and other animals in the forest.

"Plantains taste almost like roast potatoes," Joe said. "And the fish was great."

"I didn't really get it when Ed called the forest Mother in his speech at the U.N.," Frank said. "But I do now. When you're in the rain forest, it does feel somehow alive—because all the plant and animal life fit together like one huge living organism."

"I can't see why anyone would want to wreck this place," Joe said.

"What do you say we bed down now and hit the trail at first light?" Oren asked.

Nobody objected. They made a sleeping circle and fell into a deep sleep.

Early the next morning Frank woke as Joe tapped him on the shoulder. Frank rubbed his eyes. Only a hint of light had entered the forest, and the dim surroundings were almost unreal.

"Wha—" Frank said, starting to sit up.

Joe put a finger to his lips and pointed silently into the brush. Frank froze. There in the grass about twenty feet in front of them crouched a jaguar.

"Still think I was dreaming?" Joe whispered.

From the corner of his eye, Frank could see that Oren and John were awake now, too. "Oren," Frank said, quietly. "What do we do to keep him from attacking?"

"Don't move," Oren replied, motionless, not a single muscle twitching.

"Nice kitty," John said softly, keeping his eyes on the wild cat.

Frank stared, too. Almost five feet long with a sleek, massive head, the jaguar's silky black-spotted fur covered dense, powerful muscles. The creature looked as gentle as a house cat—except for its crouch and the low, ominous growl emanating from its throat.

For a long time the jaguar watched the humans. Frank tried to still his breathing and the pounding in his chest. When at last the creature loped toward the group, Frank had the eerie feeling that its green eyes were staring right into his. The jaguar came to within ten feet of the fire, then suddenly veered to the right and headed away from their camp.

"Where's it going?" Frank cried, forgetting to be quiet.

"Shh!" Oren hissed between clenched teeth.

At the noise the jaguar stopped, turned

around, and peered back at the group. Its tail twitched once, and then its mouth opened in a huge, toothy yawn. In the next instant the creature turned its back on the group and loped off through the trees.

"How about some backup, brother?" Frank asked, leaping to his feet and running toward the trees after the jaguar.

"I'm right behind you, Frank!" Joe cried. "Let's see where he's headed."

"Hey, wait! Do you want to get killed? That cat would as soon eat you as look at you!" Behind him, Frank heard John grabbing the packs and running into the forest after the Hardys. Behind him, Oren quickly doused the fire and followed.

For a few minutes Frank thrilled to the run through the dimly lit, sweet-smelling forest, leaping easily over trailing vines and dodging tree trunks and hanging orchids. Five minutes later his pace slowed as he realized that he no longer heard the crashing of the escaping jaguar ahead of him.

"We've lost him," Frank said, standing between two towering tree trunks.

"You may have lost him, but you can bet he hasn't lost us," John said, joining them and bending over to catch his breath. "He's probably lying on one of those tree branches up there right now, looking down at us and laughing, thinking what a great feast we're going to make. What kind of fool are you, Frank, running off into the forest like that?"

"I don't know." Frank looked at Joe, who was also panting from the run, and then at Oren, who had joined them looking a little winded and wan. The run had made them all hot and sweaty, and the jungle air lay on their skins like a heavy blanket. "I don't usually do stuff like this. Something got into me, and I just wanted to run—"

"Fine," John said, pushing Frank forward through the trees. "However we got here, let's keep moving. I'd rather be a moving target than a sitting duck for that jaguar—wherever he is."

John was interrupted by a shrill, earsplitting cry from off in the trees. Startled, Frank stopped again, forcing those behind him to stop as well. "What's that?" he asked.

"It sounds like a guacharo—a black bird that lives only here in Venezuela," Oren told him. "It's kind of a hawk, but the people here think of it as a demon bird—a bird of darkness."

"Why?" Joe asked.

"No idea," Oren said. "Just superstition, I guess."

"Great," Joe grumbled. "Not only are we completely lost with a jaguar on our heels, but we've got some kind of demon creature ahead of us."

Oren peered up into the trees. "My guess is that Frank and Joe scared that cat halfway to Brazil."

The bird cry sounded again.

"Then that leaves just the demon," Joe remarked.

"This isn't getting us anywhere," Frank said impatiently. "Oren, can you tell the direction we came from? Is there any way we can get back to the waterfall?"

"That should be easy," Oren replied. "We broke enough branches running here."

The group was heading slowly back toward their campsite when Joe suddenly stopped in his tracks. "Hey—what's this?" he asked, peering off to the right.

John peeked over his shoulder. "It looks like a trail," he said in disbelief.

"Well, come on. Let's see where it leads," Joe said excitedly. "It generally follows the same direction we were heading, up the river."

Joe led the way onto the narrow path, away from the clearing. The trail was narrow and half overgrown, but when it met a narrow stream, the group found a crudely built log bridge. One by one, the Hardys, Oren, and John crossed over on the slippery log and soon reached a large clearing in the forest.

"This looks a little less overgrown," Frank said. The tree canopy was thinner, and he could feel the heat from the sun getting hotter. "Why is it that the farther we go, the more lost I feel?"

"Because we *are* lost," John snapped worriedly. Just then the strange bird cry sounded again, loud enough to hurt Frank's ears. "And I think we'd better get moving unless you want to stand here and meet whatever is making that strange sound," John added.

"Let's move," Joe said, pushing forward across the clearing.

"I'm with you," Frank said, following Joe into denser forest again. "Wherever this trail leads, it's better than where we've been."

The words were hardly out of Frank's mouth when a rustling sounded from behind some trees and two men appeared on the path, blocking the men's path.

"Hey!" Frank cried, stepping back as he took in the young men's short, stocky forms, their thick, straight black hair, and the long, spearlike pointed sticks clutched in their strong brown hands. The pair wore nothing but red loincloths and black armbands decorated with parrot feathers. Their muscular chests were painted with plate-size circles and long, vertical wavy lines.

"They're Yanomama," Frank heard Oren say excitedly behind him on the path. "'We must be near their village."

As Oren spoke, one of the two young men shouted to them in his language. Stepping back, the pair ushered Frank and his companions down the narrow path. Moving past them into a large clearing, Frank was astonished to see an enormous round hut made of woven leaves and branches. The hut was as wide as a football field, yet it had been completely hidden by the forest twenty yards away. Standing in front of the hut were a dozen more Yanomama holding bows, machetes, and wooden spears.

Among them, Frank spotted Gold Tooth. He stared at Frank and Joe accusingly. Frank noticed that he wore a beaded ankle band like those in the bag of trade goods that had disappeared the same night he had. The memory of the shattered glasses flickered before Frank's eyes. Could Roger O'Neill have faced these same warriors moments before he died?

The men shouted angrily at Frank and the others in an unintelligible tongue. Several of them stepped forward, waving their spears.

"I sure hope they're giving us a hearty welcome," Joe said nervously.

"Don't bet on it," John retorted, staring at their weapons. "One false move and that jaguar will have his feast tonight after all."

Chapter

11

"WHAT DOES HE WANT?" Joe demanded as one of the Yanomama stepped forward and grabbed his arm.

"He wants us to go inside," Oren said as the group was pulled toward the large round hut. "The chief must be inside. He has to give them permission to kill us, you know."

The man who had grabbed Joe shouted again in his language. Joe didn't need a translator to understand he was being told to be quiet. He allowed himself to be shoved through an opening in the hut. Inside, he realized that the house was doughnut-shaped, with a dirt floor. Its inside wall opened onto a shady courtyard.

"What is this place?" Joe said, forgetting not to talk.

"It's called a *shapono*," Oren whispered. "Everybody in the village lives here. The roof shelters them from the weather, but they spend most of their time in the courtyard."

Joe could see that the courtyard was filled with Yanomama women, children, and older men. Some of the children were painted with circles and lines as their fathers were. They cowered close to their mothers as they stared at the strange intruders.

Just then Joe saw two old Yanomama men step forward from the shadows of the shapono. One of the men wore his hair long and tied back. His body was stained from head to toe with dark, jaguarlike spots. He stared at the strangers with sharp black eyes—and made a shrieking sound exactly like the strange bird they heard in the forest. Joe went cold as the warriors behind him shouted again.

"That's the tribal shaman, or magician," Oren murmured. "You can tell from the markings on his face."

The other man looked even older than the shaman. His skin was deeply creased and lined, and his hair was streaked with gray, but he had the same boyish face and sharp eyes as Ed's. Joe realized with a jolt that this must be Ed's father, the tribe's headman. Somehow they had stumbled onto Ed's village!

Joe flinched nervously as the shaman and the chief stepped closer. They reached out and ran their hands over Frank and Joe's hair and the fabric of their clothes. Finally the headman stepped back, clapped his hands, and barked an order. Gold Tooth stepped forward. The headman barked another order, and a third Yanomama man stepped forward. This man stood out because he had a long wispy beard—and because he could speak a little Spanish. Luckily, Oren and John spoke fluent Spanish. Gold Tooth muttered something in Yanomama.

"This man says you hurt the headman's son, Ed," Long Beard said in Spanish. John translated. "You put him in jail in the faraway world." Gold Tooth broke in and shouted, slapping his chest and shaking his fist at Frank and Joe.

"Gold Tooth says we four sent other white men to come here and take away his brother and his cousins," John said, translating Long Beard's words. "He says he tried to drown us in the Orinoco so we couldn't imprison any more."

"Incredible!" Joe said, shaking his head. "Who gave him these wild ideas?"

John asked Long Beard to ask this of Gold Tooth, who pounded his chest and yelled in Yanomama.

"He said the white men who took his brother and cousins said that you would follow," John said, translating Long Beard's Spanish. "They said you would take more Yanomama away."

"That doesn't make any sense," Joe said. "We didn't even know these guys were here."

"Of course not," Frank said. "But whoever kidnapped O'Neill must have known. They grabbed Gold Tooth's relatives and forced them to confess to the kidnapping to the Caracas police. What did the white men look like?" Frank demanded of Gold Tooth, nodding at John to translate.

Gold Tooth spat out the answer, and all the Yanomama laughed. Long Beard was still laughing as he translated into Spanish for John.

"He said all white men look like warthogs to him," John said, laughing. "He can't tell them apart."

Frank stepped forward. "Ask him what he was doing with Maddie. Did she help him break the outboard motor?"

Once again Joe and Frank waited while the question was translated, answered, and translated again. This time there was no laughter.

"He said he ran away after his relatives were dragged away," John told them. "He was afraid the men would come back for him. When he reached the mission it was abandoned, and Father Juan was gone."

"Just as Carlos Cruz said," Frank noted.

"Gold Tooth said he hid there alone," John added. "Then the rebels found him. But Maddie was there, too. She's a friend of the tribe, and she promised to help Gold Tooth get home."

"Did he tell Maddie about the men who came for the Yanomama?" Joe asked.

"Yes," John said, translating. "She said you were good men, though. Gold Tooth said he didn't believe her. He thought you had tricked Maddie, but he pretended to help you because she wanted him to."

"See!" Joe said. "Maddie didn't do it." He watched as the headman reacted to the news that Maddie had said these captives were good men.

"Ask him if Maddie told him that we're friends of Ed's," Oren said.

There was no need for translation. The headman, Ed's Father, heard the word *Ed* and the sun came up in his eyes.

"Ed," Joe said, pointing to himself. "Ed is okay."

The headman smiled, patted Joe on the back, and repeated, nodding, "Ed is okay."

The headman spoke gruffly in Yanomama. Gold Tooth answered, looking ashamed and afraid. Long Beard and John translated.

"The headman asked him why he said we hurt Ed," John said. "Gold Tooth said he just guessed we did because all outsiders are evil."

The headman clapped his hands and ordered Gold Tooth to be taken away. As he was being dragged off, he screamed in Yanomama, focusing on Joe. Long Beard translated.

"He says you're a coward and can't fight," said Oren. "He calls you Yellow Hair and says he knows you like Maddie, because you both have yellow hair."

"Right," John said. "He wants to fight for her. The winner gets Maddie."

Joe laughed. "This hair color theory is new," he said. "But I don't think Maddie would appreciate being the prize in a fight."

Gold Tooth was still shouting, but the headman barked some orders and he was led out of the shapono and into the forest. Joe was relieved. Fighting Gold Tooth was the last thing he wanted to do right then.

The headman led them to his hearth for a meal of roast plantains and small game birds. They finished eating as the sun moved past high noon.

Joe realized he was bone weary. He started to sit on the ground, but the headman showed him to one of the groups of hammocks that dotted the shapono, along with baskets, tools, and family belongings, every ten feet or so. Frank, John, and Oren got in hammocks as well. Joe's was too short, but he thought it felt luxurious after sleeping on the damp ground. He didn't even mind being stared at by the three dozen curious men, women, and children standing in the courtyard.

"This wasn't exactly a warm welcome," Joe said. "The Yanomama are pretty tough."

"They are," Oren told him. "One of the men's favorite pastimes is to hold dueling sessions. They club each other in the chest and stomach until one of them collapses or dies. But now that the rain forest is being destroyed, it's these aggressive tribes—the Yanomama and the Kayapo in Brazil—who are doing the best job of surviving."

"If anyone can do it, they can," John remarked.

Joe tried to relax, but many members of the tribe had grown braver as the strangers proved harmless. They drew closer, laughing, poking, and trying to communicate. Joe glimpsed the headman keeping an eye on the four of them through the crowd. The concern in the chief's weather-beaten face reminded Joe of the same look he had often seen on his own father's. Joe realized just then how brave Ed's father had been to send his son away for the sake of his tribe.

The headman gave Joe a gourd full of water and left him to sleep, ordering the onlookers away.

"This hammock feels great," murmured Joe. "I think I could learn to like it here."

"You know what's bothering me?" Frank asked.

"I have a feeling you're going to tell me," Joe said.

"I keep thinking about the curare-tipped dart that was found in O'Neill's car," he said. "If the Yanomama were framed—and we believe they were—who else would have access to a poison like this?"

"You're right," Joe said. "Maddie seems to be in the clear. And we heard Carlos Cruz complaining that Maddie wouldn't provide him with cu-rare. So that brings us back to the Yanomama."

"Or those cattle barons, the Da Silvas," John said.

Frank nodded. "If it was the Yanomama, then where are they keeping O'Neill?" He studied the Yanomama. Several children, having forgotten the intruders, were now skipping pebbles across the courtyard's dirt floor, while two of the warriors had resumed weaving hammocks. "He's not in this shapono or the courtyard. You can see every inch of this place from here."

"Maybe we should search the forest near here," Joe suggested.

"We'd have to be very careful," Frank said. "If they didn't snatch O'Neill, they might think we were trying to escape, or that we wanted to ambush them."

"You're right," Joe said glumly. "But at least we can get the translator to ask questions."

"Good idea," John said from deep inside his hammock. "But we've had a rough day, guys. Before we proceed, could we please get some sleep?"

Everybody agreed. As the sun drifted down-ward, they fell into a deep sleep, lulled by the daytime sounds in the village.

Slipping in and out of dreams, Joe heard little children giggling around his hammock, and he heard adults come and shoo their children away. All the sounds he heard were pleasant, and they filled his head with pleasant dreams—until he was awakened with a jolt.

"What was—" Joe yelled, sitting up and immediately twisting upside down in his hammock and falling to the floor. Gold Tooth stood over him, shrieking and swinging a heavy club.

"Hey!" Joe said, scrambling to his feet. Other Yanomama tried to pull Gold Tooth away, but he yanked himself free and ran straight for Joe.

"Joe! Watch out!" Joe heard John shout from behind him. "He's going to hit you! He's challenging you to a duel!"

Before Joe could react, Gold Tooth lifted the club with both arms and brought it down hard on Joe's chest.

Chapter

12

"GRAB THAT GUY!" Frank yelled, gesturing toward Gold Tooth as he ran toward his brother. Joe was lying on the ground beside his hammock, clutching his chest and gasping for air.

"Are you okay?" Frank asked, shaking Joe's shoulders gently.

Joe nodded, still gasping, as Oren and John grabbed Gold Tooth and wrested the club from his grip. Joe saw John reach into his waistband for the pistol Maddie had given him. But he seemed to change his mind and put it back.

Joe realized that John had done the right thing: One gunshot could turn the whole village against them. "I'm okay," Joe said weakly, getting his breath back. "Just tell him I don't accept the challenge, okay?"

Joe's voice infuriated Gold Tooth. The Yano-mama broke free from Oren's grip, grabbed his club, and pounded the ground by Joe's right foot. Joe heard the heavy club whistle by his ear as Frank instinctively leapt out of the way. Grabbing a piece of firewood, Joe held it over his head to protect himself.

With a grunt the Yanomama swung the club again, but this time Joe's thick stick deflected the blow with a crack that made him flinch. The stick fell to the ground in two useless pieces. "Somebody stop this guy!" Joe yelled at the others, who were trying to subdue the sweating and shouting warrior.

"We're trying!" Oren said. "He keeps getting away!"

As Gold Tooth came at Joe again, screaming and swinging the club over his head, Joe backed against the wall of the shapono. Out of the corner of his eye he saw another thick piece of firewood, but it was too far away. Gold Tooth stood in front of him, grinning as he grasped his club in both hands, ready to deal the second blow.

It's okay. Don't panic, Joe said to himself, sliding down the wall into a squatting position. Then, behind Gold Tooth, Joe spotted Frank with his own club taking aim at Gold Tooth's head.

An uproar erupted in the crowd. To Joe's relief, the sound caused Gold Tooth to hesitate. In that moment the tribe's headman and the shaman pushed their way into the circle.

"Stop!" the headman shouted. The word was in Yanomama but the meaning was plain. He grabbed Gold Tooth by the shoulders and flung him aside, then pushed Frank and his club away. He held out a muscular arm to Joe and pulled him to his feet. Joe was amazed at the man's strength. Ed's father looked about sixty, though Joe knew he could be forty or one hundred, it was impossible to tell. However old he was, Joe said to himself, he was glad the man had lived long enough to save his life.

As Gold Tooth was once again secured by the members of his tribe, the shaman said something in Yanomama that caused everyone in the crowd to start talking at once.

"What's going on?" Joe yelled. Watching Joe, the headman ordered Long Beard to step forward and translate. Long Beard did as he was told, and John and Oren took turns translating as well.

"The shaman says that something strange just happened," John said. "He says that while you were fighting, a giant snake, huge even for an anaconda, crawled right into the shapono. The shaman thinks it is a sign—one of many signs—that nature is out of balance."

"So what else is new?" Frank muttered, dropping his club to the floor. The shaman was now listening to two young men in the crowd who were shouting and shaking their arms. Long Beard translated into Spanish as fast as he could.

"These guys are telling him of a strange, square shapono they spotted while they were hunting," John said. "They saw it two moons—two months—ago. It didn't belong to any Yanomama tribe."

"The young men claim the square shapono had strange powers," Oren said, taking over for John. "They saw lights in the sky and heard strange sounds."

"The Yanomama who live nearby told them that the headman there has great powers," John said. "They said the headman in the strange shapono is a white man. He comes from far away."

Joe stared at John. He felt a chill run down his spine. Could it be that the kidnappers were outsiders, with a hideout deeper in the forest than anyone imagined? Unless the Yanomama were tricking them, and he doubted it, they would have to go to this strange shapono to see if O'Neill was there.

"Do the hunters know the white man's name?" Joe asked. Oren asked Long Beard, who asked the shaman. The shaman stared hard at Joe and shook his head.

Then the headman turned and yelled at Gold Tooth, who slunk off, his head hanging. The headman then ordered everyone else away and said something to Long Beard.

"The headman wants to talk to you a little later at his hearth," came the translation. "With the shaman and the young men who have been to the strange shapono."

Walking across the open area, they saw a chilling sight—a group of women were hacking apart the huge brown, tan, and black-spotted anaconda, using the machetes that Gold Tooth had stolen.

"They're going to eat that snake," Oren said.

"Even though they think it's a bad omen?" Joe asked.

"Oh, they probably debated about whether or not it was an evil spirit, but these are practical people." John laughed. "They wouldn't throw a big, tasty snake like that away without hard proof it was possessed by evil spirits."

Joe and Frank looked at each other and burst out laughing.

"Just like Aunt Gertrude," Joe said laughing.

The headman gestured for Joe, Frank, Oren, and John to sit in hammocks near his hearth. The shaman sat in the hammock closest to the fire with Long Beard and the two young hunters squatting on the ground next to him. A woman who seemed to be the headman's wife offered them food—roast plantains and chunks of roasted meat, served in a palm leaf.

"What kind of meat is this?" Joe asked.

"Haven't you ever tasted snake before?" John asked.

Joe turned pale.

"I've had rattlesnake," Oren said. "You know

what they say. The deadlier the snake, the better the taste."

The Yanomama men laughed, slapping their thighs.

"Why are they laughing?" Joe asked. "Nothing was translated." It dawned on Joe just then that everything they did was strange and funny to the Yanomama.

"You need to rest some more today," the headman said. "Tomorrow at dawn you will leave for the strange shapono. These men will guide you."

The two young men didn't seem to be happy about serving as guides.

"Ask the headman what he thinks is going on there," Joe said.

"He doesn't know," John reported. "The hunters are afraid of the place. They think it's an abode of evil spirits." The headman talked some more. "He says it's a long walk to the spot along the Siapo River, near the Brazilian border. He wants us to sleep so we can set out early tomorrow."

Abruptly the headman, the shaman, and the others stood and left. Joe was so drained from the fight that his hammock felt like the most comfortable bed in the world. "There's something very weird about this kidnapping," Joe said groggily. "The curare-tipped dart on the floor of O'Neill's car. The crashed helicopter with

O'Neill's ID. It's almost as if the kidnapper is luring us into the forest."

"Let's get some rest," Oren said. "We're going to get to the bottom of this tomorrow."

They had just settled down when a shot rang out. They leapt to their feet, stunned by such an alien sound in the forest. On all sides Yanomama were frantically pouring out of the shapono, their voices high and fearful.

"Come on!" Joe cried, leading the others out into the forest. Joe and his companions spotted the ancient shaman surrounded by the chattering villagers. The shaman pulled back a heavy branch to reveal the target of the shot.

Joe gasped. The beautiful jaguar lay dead, a bullet from a high-powered rifle having shattered its skull.

Chapter

13

"WHO WOULD DO THIS?" Frank asked.

"No Yanomama," John said softly. "They believe jaguars are almost magical." The Yanomama tribespeople stared in silence now.

"We'll never find the gunman in this brush," Oren said, squinting into the forest. "Unless he wants us to follow him."

"This is a waste," John said, disgusted. "It is nothing but someone sending us a message."

"But what message are we supposed to get?" Joe asked.

"Maybe someone wants to scare us into heading back to Caracas," Frank replied.

At dawn the next day Frank, Joe, Oren, and John set out with their two Yanomama guides.

Half an hour out they all were tired and soaked from perspiration and the light morning rain that was falling.

Frank gazed enviously at the Yanomama men, who never seemed to tire. Their movements were slow and deliberate, but they quickly outpaced Frank and the others.

Frank was amazed by their endurance. He tried to imitate their walk—with their knees slightly bent and their toes turned slightly inward. The Yanomama laughed as they watched him and the others experiment with the rain forest walk. The Yanomama exaggerated their walk until they were moving like monkeys; the others walked like monkeys, too.

As the morning passed, Frank felt better being in the jungle. Just as he was beginning to have fun, though, the Yanomama guides took off down a trail and seemed to disappear. Frank and Joe took turns calling. There was no reply.

"You don't think they've deserted us, do you?" Frank asked.

"They did seem pretty reluctant to guide us," Joe said.

"Let's just keep moving," John snapped. "If we can't trust Ed's people, we can't trust anyone."

That's just the problem, Frank thought as they continued walking. The jungle seemed to close in around them, as unfriendly as before.

They walked in grim silence for twenty minutes

until they found their Yanomama guides resting by the side of the trail. The taller of the two was serious, but the other was grinning at them.

"Well, look who's here," Oren said, breaking into a relieved smile himself. "I guess you were kidding around, huh? I don't know your names, so I'll just call you Tall and Short." The shorter man laughed and patted the ground, gesturing for everybody to rest.

Throughout the morning the pattern repeated: Tall and Short would jog ahead and wait for Frank and the others to catch up. Each time they found the Yanomama laughing, flashing their even white teeth. "Very funny," Joe grumbled when they encountered the hunters again. "I didn't know that scaring tourists was a traditional Yanomama pastime."

Soon the heat was so intense that everybody, including the Yanomama, tired. They staggered into a clearing that was like a tropical Garden of Eden. A turquoise stream ran through it, a stream with three waterfalls.

"This is as far as I go for now!" Joe said, staggering toward the water with a sigh. He stripped off his shirt and kicked off his boots and fell into the cold water with a splash. He shot up out of the water with a delighted whoop. "I'm not leaving here for a long time. I may never leave here, period!"

Frank was right behind his brother, and soon everybody was swimming. John and the young

Yanomama men had a contest catching fish with their bare hands. Tall won the contest.

"Look at the size of the fish he caught!" Oren crowed. "John, you're getting old and slow."

"What kind of fish is it?" Frank asked their guides after they had eaten it. When Tall and Short just laughed, Frank repeated the question.

"Get used to it, Frank," Joe said. "You're not going to know the names of anything you see in this place. The Yanomama might not even have a name for those fish."

"But it's so weird," Frank replied. "To live around things and not name them."

"The fish was good, right?" Joe asked.

"Excellent," Frank said.

"Would it have been more excellent if it had a name?" Joe asked.

"No," Frank said.

"There you go," Joe said. "A name has nothing to do with what's important." He turned to the Yanomama men, beaming. "See, I could live in the rain forest."

They packed up and walked on until early evening, when they came to another small clearing near a stream that was just a trickle over mossy rocks. Tall and Short took John and Oren hunting, leaving Joe and Frank with the equipment.

The men came back with a strange fruit that had thick green skin and raspberry-colored meat. It tasted a little like papaya, a little like strawberry, a little like nothing Frank had ever tasted. He loved it and wondered if he would ever taste it again.

"There are approximately two hundred fifty thousand species of higher plants in the world and two thirds of them grow in the rain forest," Oren said. "It's amazing when you think about it."

As they talked, they were suddenly plunged into darkness. They still weren't used to how quickly it got dark there. All of a sudden Frank realized how tired he was, his legs made of lead. Joe was actually groaning. Tall and Short showed them how to make hammocks by peeling down the bark of a tree. They peeled the bark on one side of a tree only, so it wouldn't die.

As they curled up in their hammocks, everyone quieted down. The fun was over. Sometime the next day they were going to arrive at the strange shapono, and they didn't know who or what would greet them.

As he lay in his hammock, Frank sorted through the facts of the case and tried to make an educated guess as to what could explain the strange shapono. He feared it could be a stronghold of Carlos Cruz's. It wasn't logical that the man would have only one camp. Perhaps the rebels were testing rockets and mortars for another attack on Caracas. Perhaps they were training revolutionaries.

Frank then started worrying that this trip could

be a Yanomama trick. Perhaps they were going to be led to O'Neill's kidnappers all right—to be captured themselves. He wasn't sure who the kidnappers could be—the Da Silva brothers, maybe? Or someone else the Hardys hadn't even heard of yet?

If it was a trap, Frank didn't think it had been set by Ed's father or the shaman. The possibilities and their consequences were keeping Frank awake.

"Joe?" Frank whispered. "You asleep?"

"Just about," murmured Joe.

"Do you think someone with a high-powered rifle could be standing out in the bush right now, watching us?"

"Gee, thanks for mentioning that, Frank," Joe snapped, sitting up in his bark hammock. "Now I'm wide awake. What made you think of that?"

"The jaguar that was shot," Frank said. "I wonder if it was meant as a warning to scare us off."

"I think it was probably a big game hunter who hadn't spotted the shapono," Joe answered. "When he heard people screaming, he just took off."

Then Frank heard Joe sigh in the pitch-black. "Try to think of something normal," Joe suggested. "Something from Bayport."

"I'll try," Frank said sleepily. "But this place is about as far from Bayport as we could get."

* * *

The Yanomama guides woke the Hardys and their friend early the next morning. Late in the afternoon the air grew even heavier and damper than usual. As the group emerged from the trees into an open, savannahlike patch in the forest, Frank saw that the sky had turned the color of a serious bruise—yellow and scarlet and purple and green. Thunder rumbled in the distance. A big storm was likely to hit any minute.

As he stood there focusing on the sky, Frank heard a tiny click and saw Short pitch forward and fall a few feet ahead of him.

"What happened?" Oren called from behind Frank.

Kneeling down, Frank checked the ground. "It's some kind of trip wire," he told the others as John dived for the spot where the wire ended.

"Grenade!" John yelled, grabbing a small egg-shaped object from the underbrush and pitching it as far as he could into the forest.

A moment later the jungle shook and smoke billowed up from the grenade's explosion. Dozens of birds took off in a panic of squawks and feathers. Oren, the Hardys, and the Yanomama stared at the trees, astonished. Everything had happened so fast.

"Nice pitch, John," Oren said.

"The question now is," Frank said, glancing around quickly, "who set up that trip wire and the grenade—and where are they now?"

Frank's question was interrupted by Short yelling in Yanomama. Frank followed Short's frightened gaze to see four soldiers hurrying toward them, in brand-new khaki uniforms and carrying high-powered rifles.

Without a word the soldiers stopped and leveled their rifles at Frank, Joe, and the others.

Chapter

14

"I HAVE A FEELING these guys aren't on our side," Joe said, noticing then that the men were Yanomama. They had the same short, stocky build as most of the members of Ed's tribe, and they looked so uncomfortable in their uniforms that Joe would have laughed if one of the men hadn't jabbed him in the ribs with the barrel of his rifle right then.

The man then jerked Joe's hands above his head and frisked him for weapons. The soldier appeared so tense that Joe was afraid he'd be killed if he made a wrong move. Another soldier found the pistol Maddie had given John and brandished it in the air as he shoved John down. Meanwhile, Tall and Short tried to talk to the soldiers, but the guards refused to answer. They just yelled the same thing over and over and made slashing motions across their throats.

"Basically, these guys are saying shut up or we all die," Joe guessed. "Something has them terrified." One of the soldiers screamed at him. Joe didn't understand the words, but he knew it meant "zip it up."

With their hands behind their heads, Joe and the others marched single file across the patch of grassland. As they reentered the forest, it started to pour. Curtains of water sifted down through the treetops, cutting the prisoners off even from one another.

Joe couldn't see the enormous square shapono until he was a yard from the front door. Over the sound of the rain, he heard their captors shouting in Yanomama and guessed he was supposed to enter. As he stepped inside the hollow shapono, he saw another square building almost filling the inside courtyard. A small helicopter sat on a heliport on its roof.

Joe realized that the building would be visible from the air. From outside at ground level, however, the shapono was hardly recognizable.

The guards shouted again, and Joe and the others were nudged forward and forced to climb the concrete steps of the building. Inside was what looked like a millionaire's mountain hideaway in the United States. The furniture was new and expensive; the chairs were teak with buttery leather seats. Navajo rugs were scattered around, covering wall-to-wall straw matting.

What stood out, however, was the clutter. Books and cartons of papers and brand-new coffeemakers and appliances of all kinds covered every surface. Joe knew there must be at least one generator for the air conditioner and appliances. Newspapers and magazines from all over the world were heaped on a long ebony dining room table. Yanomama baskets, blowpipes from Guyana, and Native American sacred objects from every tribe were scattered around like toys. Tall and Short looked as frightened as if they had been kidnapped and taken aboard an alien spaceship.

"I thought you'd never get here."

The voice was so familiar it sent tingles down Joe's spine. He whirled around and found himself face-to-face with Harvey Brinkman, the importer he'd met in New York. Joe was so shocked, his mind went blank. Brinkman was the last person he'd expected to run into in the rain forest.

Brinkman swaggered toward them, his lip curled into a sneer, and his pale hazel eyes stretched open wide with excitement.

"Look who we have here!" Brinkman said. Joe heard the cruel taunting in his voice "Not that it's any big surprise. My employer was expecting you sooner, actually."

"Your employer?" Joe looked around the complex. There was no sign of another person.

Then Joe noticed a copy of the *New York Times*, open to the story of O'Neill's disappearance, and a copy of Burgerworld's annual report.

Abruptly Joe recalled the cracked and stained eyeglasses in the forest and the helicopter that had been so badly concealed. Yes, he realized excitedly—it was all starting to add up.

"You used to work for O'Neill, didn't you, Harvey?" Joe said carefully. He looked at Frank, and a spark of understanding came into the older Hardy's eyes.

"You never quit working for O'Neill," Frank added. "He's here and the kidnappers aren't. In fact, there never were any kidnappers."

Joe glanced at the guards, still aiming their rifles, and bravely finished the thought. "Because he engineered his own kidnapping, and you helped!"

"What did you say?" John Tsosie roared behind Joe.

Brinkman laughed. "Bright boys," he said. "We've been working on this place for two months. The Venezuelan police were so sure it was Ed and the Yanomama who kidnapped Roger that they didn't even think it could be a scam. The idiots! And, Oren, you thought my importing business was just a moneymaking scam," he added. "If nothing else, it introduced me to people who could sell me curare and Yanomama darts."

Oren shook his head solemnly. "Harvey, I was

never your biggest fan, but I wouldn't have thought even you would be low enough to help O'Neill pull off something like this."

"It's business, Oren," Brinkman said flatly. "This land can be worth billions—do you realize that? If O'Neill doesn't get rich off it, someone else will."

"You wanted to get rich? Then why the fake kidnapping?" Joe asked, confused.

Brinkman chuckled. "The kidnapping was a brilliant idea—all Mr. O'Neill's, of course. It seems he had secretly, er, 'borrowed' several million dollars from Burgerworld and was beginning to worry that his stockholders might find out and get upset. He decided to duck out before the loss was discovered."

"O'Neill robbed his own company? He sent an innocent man to prison just so he could make more millions? I can't believe this guy, Harvey," John said in shock. "And you helped him. You're as bad as he is!"

Harvey clicked his tongue. "John, it's not polite to insult your host."

"Where is he, Harvey?" Oren asked harshly. "We nearly got killed trying to find this guy. I want you to take us to him now."

Brinkman eyed the professor coldly. "With pleasure," he said. He snapped his fingers and ordered the guards to lead the Hardys, John, and Oren to the back of the house. The terrified Yanomama guides were led outside to be put to work.

As Frank and Joe watched, one of the guards pushed Tall and Short toward the building's front door. Joe could tell their two friends were pleading for mercy in Yanomama.

"You wouldn't have gotten this far if that idiot I hired in New York had fixed your plane like I told him," Brinkman said. "You'd be ashes, and I wouldn't have to deal with you. I really hate being the bad guy, you know?"

"But money talks," John muttered.

"It's a dog-eat-dog world," Brinkman said matter-of-factly.

"That's why you were in New York," Joe said, half to himself. "O'Neill sent you to make sure Ed was arrested."

"I was keeping tabs on everybody who visited Ed," Brinkman bragged. "I had a feeling that you and your brother Frank could be trouble, and I knew that nosy Oren here would butt in. He never could pass up a good mystery."

"You hired that guy to push me in front of the subway train," Joe said.

"I was right about you," Brinkman replied. "You are bright, and absolutely correct. I had one of my men stake out Maddie's apartment until you all left. I had told him to push Oren, but he got confused. Oh, well. Before you question me any more, let me just take credit for all your little mishaps of late." Brinkman turned on his heel and stalked out of the room. "The trunk in front of Oren's apartment was mine, obviously. Who else in New York had access to a Yanomama arrow? The dead jaguar was our way of luring you here once you'd proved too stubborn to go away."

"And O'Neill's glasses? And his ID in the chopper?"

"Oh, that." Brinkman laughed. "For that, we have other plans."

At Brinkman's signal the guard pushed Joe and the others down a cream-colored hallway until they came to a locked metal door, where yet another Yanomama guard stood.

Brinkman grabbed the guard's keys and pushed him to one side. He unlocked the heavy door, which swung open slowly.

"You're about to meet an amazing man, a visionary," Brinkman said, ushering the group in.

"Right. A meal ticket," Joe grumbled.

"So amazing he hired you," Frank added. "No thanks, I think I'll pass."

"Come now," said a strange, deep voice from inside the room. "Aren't you the least bit curious about the man you came all this way to find?"

"Roger O'Neill," Joe said dully, entering the room. The man whom they'd believed had been kidnapped sat with his back to them in a big leather chair like that of an English lord. The air conditioner in this room was set even colder than in the rest of the building. Huge blue and green satellite maps of Yanomama territory were framed on the walls, and a wide-screen TV was tuned to CNN. There were bookcases stuffed with thrillers and stacks of the latest videos. Off in the corner sat another man, a pale, blond man in aviator sunglasses and a battered leather jacket.

The guards pushed Joe and the others over toward the Burgerworld chieftain.

"Gotcha!" O'Neill said. "Or did you get me? You certainly were persistent." O'Neill was tall and tan, elegant in soft, loose cotton clothes. He looked different from his newspaper photo, Joe realized—leaner, older, and certainly more evil.

"Sit down," O'Neill ordered. Chairs materialized, carried by servants who seemed to hover everywhere. Joe was no longer surprised that they were Yanomama. "Can I get anybody a drink?"

No one answered. O'Neill was obviously used to being in the company of powerful men, Joe realized. He was probably a hundred times more dangerous than Brinkman.

"This is my pilot, Tony," O'Neill said. The blond man in the corner looked at them without expression. "So nice of him to join our little team. Unfortunately, we lost our last pilot in a little helicopter crash."

"Tell me, Mr. O'Neill," Oren said. "How does it feel to be kidnapped by dangerous Yanomama? Did they poison you or just shoot you with arrows?"

O'Neill dropped the charm and went hard and

cold. "My brother was killed by natives in the Amazon. I have no great love for 'native people.' Their ways can be as murderous as anyone else's."

"Nobody knows what happened to your brother, Mr. O'Neill," Oren said. "But—"

"Let's not waste time," O'Neill said. "As you can see, I have much to do."

"Yes, you have no idea how big Mr. O'Neill's plans are. These gold mines—"

"Shut up, Harvey!" O'Neill snapped.

"Mines?" Frank said. "You're using the money you stole from Burgerworld to mine for gold here in virgin rain forest territory? Do you know what that will do to the people and wildlife here?"

"Don't take this as an insult, Mr. O'Neill," Joe said tightly, "but that sounds a little greedy."

O'Neill grinned. He had a long, gaunt face and long teeth, and he looked like a wolf when he smiled.

"This is beyond greed, boy," he said. "This is an act that's going to show the world who Roger J. O'Neill really is." He sat back in his chair. "It's time to take these boys to their room."

The guard prodded and pushed the captives out a back door. After the artificial cold of O'Neill's bunker, the heat surprised Joe. Now that the rain had stopped, he could see that behind the building the courtyard of the shapono was filled with crates, boxes, and equipment of all kinds. According to their labels, the crates contained medical and kitchen supplies; three-wheeled motorcycles and bicycles leaned against the crates; and all around were cement mixers, stacks of two-by-fours, an earth mover, and a huge tank of diesel fuel.

Behind the construction equipment was another, much smaller, windowless concrete building. Their march ended there. They were hustled up the flight of metal steps and through a door, only to face another steel door with a big prison lock. Joe got a sinking feeling in his stomach.

"This looks very bad," Joe heard John murmur as the guard opened the steel door. The cell inside was pitch black. The guard looked at Joe and snickered, and the next thing Joe knew he was tasting sawdust. An instant later the others landed on the floor beside him as the guard slammed the door.

"Frank," Joe called. He could hear huge insects skittering around on the concrete floor.

"Over here, Joe," Frank said. "I'm waving. Can you see my hand?"

"*Nada,* zip, nothing," Joe replied. "It's as dark as the inside of a cow, as Aunt Gertrude says. Oren, John, you still with us?"

"Be quiet and listen!" Oren said.

Joe did as he was told. Almost immediately he heard a soft moaning coming from the corner of the cell.

Chapter

15

FRANK MADE IT to the moaning prisoner before any of the others could. He was curled up in the corner, shirtless, and shivering in spite of the heat. "Who are you?" Frank asked.

"Father Juan, from the mission on the Orinoco," the prisoner mumbled. Frank could barely make out what he was saying.

"Don't try to talk," Frank said. Without thinking about what he was doing, he took off his shirt and wrapped it around the frail, elderly priest. Walker crawled over and felt Father Juan's forehead.

"He's trembling and has a high fever. He's got malaria," Oren said. "We have to get him some medicine."

"I bet he hasn't had anything to eat for days," Frank said. "Hey, Joe? Oren? John?"

"Yeah?" Joe asked.

"No amount of money in the world is enough to make a man treat another man this way."

"They are starving me," Father Juan mumbled. "That fat American, Brinkman, said they had to make me thin so that I would make a perfect skeleton."

"A what?" Frank cried. "What did he mean, a skeleton?"

"They kidnapped me because I am about the same height and weight as O'Neill," the priest explained. "The fat man said he was going to pay an official to switch our dental records."

"So your skeleton would be identified as O'Neill's," Frank said, disgusted. "And then everyone would believe Roger O'Neill was dead."

"And that the Yanomama had killed him," Joe added, sitting back against the cell wall. His voice was calm and deadly. "They're not going to get away with this."

Day melted into night. Frank only guessed it was night because he was so hungry.

As the hours wore on, thirst got the upper hand. Father Juan drifted in and out of sleep. Just being with others seemed to give him a little more strength.

"Frank! Did you hear that! An explosion!"

Frank woke up on the floor and wondered if Father Juan was still alive. He felt happy when he heard the soft breathing beside him.

"Frank! Wake up and listen! Another explosion!"

Frank heard two explosions. He sat up. Beside him, Father Juan tried to sit up, too. Through the thick walls they could hear a lot of shouting and running and sharp cracks that sounded like gunfire.

"Who do you think it is? The police? The Yanomama?" Frank asked.

The door opened with a bang before Joe could answer. The morning light was blinding. Hands and forearms shot up to cover eyes. Looking between his fingers, Frank made out the outline of a woman being held by two guards. "Maddie Hatfield?" he cried.

As the guards, blinded by darkness, carried Maddie kicking and screaming into the room, Joe crawled across the floor to the door. While the guards had their backs turned, Frank watched Joe tear a strip of cloth from the tail of his shirt and stuff it into the lock.

The guards shoved Maddie down so hard that she bounced off the wall. Joe's leg went out like a shot as the guards were backing out with their guns drawn. Frank kicked the shin of one of the guards who then fell backward over Joe's leg. He went down firing. The sound was deafening in the confined space. The bullets simply punched holes in the ceiling without doing any real damage. Quickly the guard scrambled to his feet. He and his partner backed out into the light, yelling warnings. They slammed the prison door, but to Frank's relief they didn't seem to notice that the lock failed to click shut.

"I think their consciences are bothering them," Frank said dryly.

Maddie didn't laugh. She had found Father Juan.

"He's burning up," she said. "I have antimalaria tablets, antibiotics, and painkillers in my waist pack. I have a canteen, too. The idiots didn't have time to take anything but my gun away. Here, help me sit him up."

Gently John pulled the priest up to a sitting position.

"Father Juan, it's Maddie," she said. "Take this medicine, Father. It'll get rid of the fever."

"Ah, Maddie," the priest said. "Good girl. You always did know what to do."

After the priest drank, Maddie passed around the canteen. The water was warm but it tasted better than anything Frank had ever drunk.

Outside, the cracks and pops of gunfire were coming closer together.

"Maddie, do you mind telling us what's happening out there?" Joe said.

"The Red Shirts are shooting the place up," she told him. "Lucky for us, Carlos hates O'Neill more than he hates you guys. I convinced him you were okay. It's safe."

"Lucky for us?" John said. "Maddie, that guy hates us almost as much as O'Neill."

"Listen, I'd love to stay and chat," Frank said. "But let's get out of here. Those guards could come back any minute and notice that the lock doesn't work."

"Frank's right," Oren said. "Look, John, we're just going to have to trust her. Frank, why don't you and John carry Father Juan?"

To Frank's relief, Father Juan seemed cooler already, and he was resting easier. Even asleep, he was as light as a child. Frank knew that the priest would have to get medical attention fast or he would die.

As Frank and John reached the door with the half-conscious priest, he saw a crack of light appear around the unlocked steel door. Joe was pressing lightly on the slab of metal. He glanced at his older brother and said, "Let's go."

Even before his eyes got used to the light, Frank realized they had stepped into chaos. Young rebels in red shirts zigzagged across the open area, shooting at Yanomama in khaki shirts. Joe emerged from the prison and headed for two big crates, Maddie and Oren right behind him. A red shirt on the roof of the prison drew a bead on Joe until he noticed Maddie and lowered his gun.

"That was close," said John. "Now it's our turn."

Frank and John dragged Father Juan to the crates and laid the priest carefully behind one before crouching down beside Joe and Maddie and Oren.

"I don't see Brinkman or O'Neill anywhere!" Frank shouted over the noise. "I'm sure they're locked up safe and sound in the big house."

"Real heroes," Oren said.

"We've got to get Father Juan into the house," Frank said. "They've got major medical supplies in there."

A bullet whistled overhead.

"Medical supplies but no doctor," John said. "Great."

"I can take care of him," Maddie said.

"Maddie, he's not a plant," John snapped.

"I'm trained as a doctor," Maddie told him. "That's how I met Carlos."

Frank stared at her. "John told us you went to medical school," he said. "But Carlos went, too? That's a shock."

"We both started out caring for people," Maddie said, squinting up at the red shirt on the roof. "In our own ways we both still do."

A bullet smacked into the corner of the crate, splintering it.

"We better get in there now," Joe said. "Or O'Neill will bolt." His face was hard. "Do we go together or what?" He was looking at Frank.

"No choice, brother," Frank said. "Father Juan isn't going to stay alive out here."

They ran. The first big surprise was that the door to the concrete house was unlocked. It flashed through Joe's mind that O'Neill or Brinkman might have left it open to lure the others inside.

"More guards should be around here somewhere," Oren said. "They probably closed ranks around their fearless leader."

"We'll just have to stay out of their way," Joe said. "And keep away from the Red Shirts, too."

But there were no Red Shirts inside the building. Instead, the Hardys found Harvey Brinkman standing on a chair in the hallway that led to O'Neill's wing. He was alternately pounding on the door with his fists and trying to smash open the transom above it with his fists.

"He locked me out!" Brinkman howled when he saw the Hardys. "He left me here alone to deal with the savages!"

"Savages?" Joe said in a dead calm voice. "Do you see this priest? Whoever denied him food and medicine is the savage. Who did it, Brinkman?"

"What did you expect?" Brinkman shrieked in a panic. "We had to show them what would happen to them if they tried to run away. They don't understand English!"

"You did it to scare the Yanomama," Oren

said. "And to get a corpse. You're the savage, Brinkman."

"Don't hurt me," Brinkman pleaded, crumpling on to his chair.

"About what I expected," John said. "Sit up straight."

Brinkman did as he was told. Meanwhile, Joe grabbed a discarded rifle and shot the lock to O'Neill's sanctuary off after five or six tries.

Rushing inside, the Hardys found the main room empty.

"Over here!" John said, opening a door in the far corner of the room.

Frank and Joe raced toward the door. Inside, they found what they guessed was O'Neill's bedroom, with a luxurious king-size bed, banks of television sets, and a portable kitchen. O'Neill could hole up here for months in an emergency, Frank realized. To his relief, there was a cabinet in the corner stocked with sterile bandages and other medical supplies.

"Perfect!" Frank said. "Maddie can take care of Father Juan here. Oren, you stay here with Brinkman."

"My pleasure," Oren said grimly. "I'll tie his wrists with the cords from his own native masks."

The sound of gunfire had faded back into the surrounding forest. Frank guessed that O'Neill's Yanomama guards and servants were luring the Red Shirts away from O'Neill according to orders. The sudden noise of whirring helicopter rotors rising above that of the battle told Frank where O'Neill was right then. Leaving Father Juan with Maddie and Oren, Frank raced out of the room toward the back door. John and Joe followed as Frank scrambled up an outdoor ladder to the roof. The wind from the rotors almost knocked him over as he stood at the top of the ladder.

Frank was not surprised to see O'Neill, surrounded by four rifle-bearing Yanomama, making his way to the helicopter. His pilot, Tony, was sitting at the controls. Almost immediately, one of the guards spotted Frank and aimed at him. With a yell Frank hit the deck. In a second Joe and John were beside him. "Use the rifle, Joe!" Frank shouted over the noise of the chopper.

Frank felt his heart hammering in his ears as Joe took aim and shot the rear rotor, crippling the machine. The engine sputtered and died as O'Neill spun on his heel, yelling for his men to go after the attackers.

"Run!" Joe yelled, backing toward the ladder. Frank, John, and Joe half slid, half fell back down to the ground. At the bottom John took Joe's rifle and dropped into a combat stance. When two of the bodyguards peeked over the edge, he shot the guns right out of their hands.

"Nice shooting, partner," Frank said, impressed.

"My pleasure," John responded with a tight smile. Leaning back to look up at the roof again, he shouted, even though he knew they didn't understand, "Come on, boys, time to line up with your hands in the air. And tell your boss to come down easy. If we don't get any more trouble from him, he may just live long enough to stand trial back home."

"I'm coming!" The voice from the roof sounded old and weak. "My pilot will follow."

Frank stared at John and Joe as O'Neill hobbled down the ladder, carrying a single black briefcase. His face was gaunt and pale. He seemed to have aged twenty years since the Red Shirts arrived. The burger czar reached the dusty ground and hobbled toward the Hardys and John, his cold eyes boring into them all.

Then, unexpectedly, he took a hard left and began running as fast as he could around the edge of the building.

"Hey!" Frank shouted. "He's getting away!"

Chapter

16

JOHN FIRED a warning shot into the air, but the noise didn't slow their quarry for an instant. Frank, Joe, and John raced after O'Neill, who was clearly hoping to escape through the shapono's main entrance. Just as Frank rounded the last corner of the building, he saw Roger O'Neill stop abruptly and howl in rage.

Standing in the entrance to the shapono were Helena, Matt, Sogyal, and a young woman with a portable video camera. Beside them was a satellite dish about four and a half feet across. And the camera was aimed at Roger O'Neill.

"Smile, Roger!" the camera operator shouted. "You're on the six-thirty news!"

"What?" Frank said as Joe and John rounded the corner behind them. "What's going on?"

145

"Hey, guys!" Matt shouted. "How do you like our portable satellite dish? We caught that whole scene on the rooftop and beamed it live to New York. This brilliant network camera operator, Melissa Jenkins, hooked up the whole thing."

"Listen, Matt," Melissa said, panning with the camera as she spoke. "Don't call me brilliant again if you want to live. And Susan helped a lot, you know."

"Who's Susan?" Frank turned toward the main building in time to see Susan Levy, a correspondent he recognized from the network news. She was exiting the building with Oren and Harvey Brinkman. Brinkman's hands were tied, and he looked mortified.

"I had no idea Mr. O'Neill stole funds from Burgerworld," Brinkman protested loudly as Melissa aimed the camera at him. "I honestly thought he was building a retreat and a center for research on the Yanomama and the rain forest."

As he talked, Melissa slowly panned to the forest behind her. Frank saw with surprise that the tribe of Yanomama from Ed's village were hovering in the shadows of the trees, staring at Brinkman in fear and horror. Among them, Frank was relieved to see, were Tall and Short.

The headman, Ed's father, emerged from the shadows. Melissa's camera followed him as he crossed into the courtyard and up to Maddie. With great ceremony he embraced her.

Frank was so shocked that for a moment he

had forgotten all about Roger O'Neill. Melissa hadn't. She captured him as he ran up to Brinkman and tried to strangle him with his long, bony fingers.

"I should have known better than to listen to you, you fruitcake!" he shrieked. "Now everything is up in smoke! I could kill you!"

Nobody moved for a minute or two. Slowly O'Neill became aware that the camera was on him. He buried his face in his hands.

"I guess you wonder how we found you here," Matt said, appearing with Sogyal at Frank's side.

"Well, yes, actually. I was wondering that," Joe said casually, keeping his eyes on O'Neill.

"Ed's dad led us to you," Sogyal explained. Helena got worried when she kept radioing Father Juan's mission and could never reach him. Finally she flew to the mission and found no one there. So she asked us to go along with her to Ed's village to find out what happened to you guys. It was Helena's idea to get a news crew to come."

"Yeah, but it was you who thought about calling the American networks, Matt," Sogyal said loyally. "If we'd had just a local crew, Americans wouldn't have been able to see their burger lord trying to run away from his rescuers while his bodyguards were trying to kill them!"

"O'Neill kidnapped himself, you know," Joe said grimly. "He'd embezzled from his company

147

and planned to use the money to mine for gold here."

Sogyal nodded. "We were beginning to piece together some of that from the action we saw on the roof."

Just then Frank heard the sound of approaching helicopters. "What's that?" he asked, instantly on the alert.

Sogyal smiled. "The Venezuelan police, of course," he said. "Helena's one smart cookie. She called them before we called the news."

Helena Vargas's cool, white hilltop house looked like a palace after the jungle. Joe and Frank stood looking out Helena's picture window, watching the lights come on in the valley below. Behind them, people ate and laughed, and candles glowed and music played. It seemed as if everybody in Caracas had seen the live footage of Roger O'Neill and Harvey Brinkman at the shapono two days before, and everybody wanted to hear the story from the people involved.

The party really took off when the United States ambassador to Venezuela showed up to congratulate Frank, Joe, Oren, and John—and to tell them that Ed had been released and was flying home.

"You have prevented a grave injustice from being committed," the ambassador said. He was a handsome man who spoke in hushed, sincere tones, as if he was telling a secret he had never told anyone before.

Helena Vargas swept up as he was talking and laughed. "And what does that tell you about our own police, Mr. Ambassador?" she asked with a dazzling smile. "They were a little slow to investigate, weren't they?"

The ambassador agreed that the matter should be checked out.

"How long do you think O'Neill will get?" Frank had asked.

"Well, thanks to the worldwide television coverage," Helena said, "he can't get off easily—even if he tries to bribe everybody in sight."

Still looking out over Caracas, Joe saw Melissa Jenkins reflected in the picture window. She was talking with Matt, Helena, and Sogyal. Joe turned to join them.

"I think we make a good team," Matt was saying. "Helena, maybe you and Sogyal and I should go into the news business. What do you think, Melissa?"

She shook her head, but she was smiling.

"How did you guys get that satellite dish in there, anyway, Melissa?" Joe asked.

"It breaks down into two boxes about as big as trunks," Melissa said. "We were able to backpack them in. It was easy to set it up at O'Neill's shapono while all the shooting was going on. The dish ran on a little portable generator that one of the guys carried in. Of course, I didn't realize

O'Neill had those monster generators powering his air conditioners. I could have hooked up to one of those."

"This is the kind of satellite relay they use for all those live stories from war zones and stuff," Matt said. "The dish we had in the jungle is called the uplink. They have a downlink dish that catches the transmission right on the roof of the network building in New York City. Cool, huh?"

"Definitely cool, Matt," Joe said. "Because of you guys, Roger O'Neill and Harvey Brinkman are in jail today."

As he spoke, Maddie Hatfield joined them, a glass of punch in her hand. Joe thought she looked especially beautiful wearing a long tunic woven of native fabric.

"Hey, guys," she said to Melissa and the others. "That was great work you did out there. Ed's father asked me to thank you. The rain forest that O'Neill didn't get to destroy thanks you, too."

Joe studied Maddie's face. "Tell me, Maddie," he asked. "How did you find that place?"

"I was taking some of the Red Shirts out to search for plants," she said. "We saw pieces of your boat floating around the rapids, so I was afraid you'd drowned. Then we searched for you.

"Anyway," she continued, "we went on to Ed's village to look for you. The Yanomama were afraid of the Red Shirts—and afraid of you—but

Ed's father is an old friend of mine. He managed to let me know you were alive."

"Apparently, the film crew and I got to the village just hours after Maddie left," Helena added. "Ed's father told me that Maddie was frantic to find you."

"Cards on the table, Maddie. What were you doing with that guy Carlos?" Joe asked.

"Cards on the table, Joe. I thought I was helping to save the rain forest," Maddie said. "I've known Carlos for a long time, since medical school. We were close until he came back here and got so radical."

"But you stayed in touch," Frank said.

"Not for a long time," Maddie said. "But I knew what he was up to. I knew he believed he was fighting injustice, working to create a better world. But he didn't care about the forest. So I made a deal with him. I would show him how to obtain medicines from the plants in the forest, and he—"

"Yes?" Joe interrupted as John Tsosie also joined the party, curious to hear what the conversation was about. "What was his part of the deal?"

"He promised to leave the Yanomama in peace," she admitted. "I could ignore Carlos's politics. But I couldn't ignore the way he had been threatening the tribes."

"So why take off without telling Ed, skipping out on the U.N. conference?" John asked testily.

"That was part of the deal," Maddie told him. "Carlos got to decide when I came, and I couldn't tell anybody, or the deal was off. In any case, it's over," she added. "Carlos was rounded up along with most of his Red Shirts. Now that they're caught, they'll be in jail for quite a while."

There were shouts of excitement behind them. Joe spun around to see that Ed Yanomama had just walked in. Oren rushed over from another corner of the room and locked his friend in a bear hug. John was right beside him. It took Frank and Joe a second to register that their dad, Fenton, was with Ed, too. Without thinking, they ran across the room.

"Boy, am I glad to see you guys," Fenton said, locking them in one giant hug. "Your mother still hasn't gotten over seeing you on the news."

"Well, we've got some good stories for her when she recovers," Joe said.

"Thanks, guys," Ed said. "I don't know how I can ever repay you."

"Listen, being in the rain forest was an amazing experience," Frank said. "It taught us a lot."

"Right," said Joe. "It taught us not to make a move when army ants march across your chest. And not to run after any jaguars."

"And that it's okay to eat a fish even if you don't know its name," added Frank.

"Well, it's good to hear you learned something," John said with a laugh.

"You know, in the Iroquois tradition," Oren

said, "a chief was supposed to make decisions with the seventh generation in mind. He tried never to do anything to the land or water that would hurt his children's children's children's children's children's children."

"Whoa," Joe said. "Imagine thinking that far into the future every time you did anything."

Everybody laughed quietly and turned to watch the darkness fall in the valley. To Joe, the lights in the houses looked like thousands of tiny campfires.

"Hey, Frank?" Joe asked softly.

"Yeah?" his brother responded.

"Promise me something," Joe said. "Don't try to drag me into the great outdoors for a long, long time."

Frank laughed. "You got it," he replied.

Frank and Joe's next case:

In an effort to protect the environment, the students of Bayport High have organized a massive recycling campaign—Project Planet Earth. Even the industrial giant United Plastics has expressed support for the idea. But someone has developed a different plan—a campaign of sabotage designed to poison the entire project.

Frank and Joe's investigation turns urgent when the dirty tricks turn deadly. A United Plastics security guard is crushed in a factory machine, and the Hardys uncover evidence of blackmail and murder. But they won't be able to prove a thing until they put their *own* lives at risk . . . penetrating the company's defenses and uncovering the darkest, dirtiest secret of all . . . in *Toxic Revenge,* Case #83 in The Hardy Boys Casefiles™.